Glenda

Praise for the Scotia MacKinnon mysteries

The Dead Wives Society

"A likable, well-developed character. This mystery is by far the most engaging thus far. . . . The conclusion is very satisfying. Anyone meeting Scotia for the first time will be eager to seek out her earlier cases and will look forward to more from the misty Northwest."   —The Mystery Reader

"Sharon Duncan has done it again." —Michael A. Hawley

A Deep Blue Farewell

"Satisfyingly complex with unexpected twists."
—The Mystery Reader

"The characters are interesting and well depicted, the portrayal of the scene and the boat culture is accurate and involving. This is an exploration of the complex ties people develop with each other, and these relationships are thoughtful and well developed."   —I Love a Mystery

"A nicely told tale. Ms. Duncan does a good job of showing the scut work that a PI faces. Scotia's interactions with her daughter are also interesting—a pleasant read."
—Romantic Times

Death on a Casual Friday

"Move over, Millhone. There's a new girl in town. [Scotia MacKinnon] is the most believable new private eye in half a dozen years. . . . The action unfolds with wit, grace, and tension, and the climax . . . is gripping."
—Joe Gores

"Fans of female P.I.s are going to cheer the arrival of Scotia MacKinnon. Appealing and intelligent, she's a welcome addition to the ranks." —Romantic Times

"[Duncan] has hit a lev
books to achieve."

"You'll love this snapp

Other Books in the Scotia MacKinnon Mystery Series

Death on a Casual Friday

A Deep Blue Farewell

The Dead Wives Society

THE LAVENDER BUTTERFLY MURDERS

A SCOTIA MacKINNON MYSTERY

SHARON DUNCAN

A SIGNET BOOK

SIGNET
Published by New American Library, a division of
Penguin Group (USA) Inc., 375 Hudson Street,
New York, New York 10014, U.S.A.
Penguin Books Ltd, 80 Strand,
London WC2R 0RL, England
Penguin Books Australia Ltd, 250 Camberwell Road,
Camberwell, Victoria 3124, Australia
Penguin Books Canada Ltd, 10 Alcorn Avenue,
Toronto, Ontario, Canada M4V 3B2
Penguin Books (NZ), cnr Airborne and Rosedale Roads,
Albany, Auckland 1310, New Zealand

Penguin Books Ltd, Registered Offices:
80 Strand, London WC2R 0RL, England

First published by Signet, an imprint of New American Library,
a division of Penguin Group (USA) Inc.

First Printing, August 2004
10 9 8 7 6 5 4 3 2 1

Copyright © Sharon Duncan, 2004
All rights reserved

 REGISTERED TRADEMARK—MARCA REGISTRADA

Printed in the United States of America

PUBLISHER'S NOTE
This is a work of fiction. Names, characters, places, and incidents either
are the product of the author's imagination or are used fictitiously, and
any resemblance to actual persons, living or dead, business establishments,
events, or locales is entirely coincidental.

BOOKS ARE AVAILABLE AT QUANTITY DISCOUNTS WHEN USED TO PROMOTE PROD-
UCTS OR SERVICES. FOR INFORMATION PLEASE WRITE TO PREMIUM MARKETING DIVI-
SION, PENGUIN GROUP (USA) INC., 375 HUDSON STREET, NEW YORK, NEW YORK 10014.

For Joplin and Nacho,
who suffered the worst that men can inflict.

PART 1

Is it in heaven, a crime to love too well?
                                    —Alexander Pope

1

I've never solved a murder in Mesopotamia, nor do I cultivate rare orchids. I enjoy a chilled dry vermouth and soda when the sun has fallen decently over the yardarm, but I've never resorted to the seven-percent solution. My name is Scotia MacKinnon. As a female gumshoe in the tiny Pacific Northwest village of Friday Harbor, I do resort to dogged determination, some well-honed law enforcement skills, a smidgen of luck, and early morning epiphanies. Despite all of these, the Dei Fiori case was the most puzzling I've encountered in two decades of law enforcement and private investigation.

My sojourn at the yoga retreat on neighboring Santa Maria Island was intended to be a vacation for seven days in May. Perhaps, strolling about the old stone courtyard with its clay pots of red geraniums and diaphanous azure butterflies, I was reluctant to recognize the incidents that plagued the retreat at the old Franciscan convent for what they were: a bizarre confluence of seemingly unrelated events that had been set in motion long before we gathered in Il Refugio with Joseph for *asanas* and readings from Rumi.

Even now, reclining in *DragonSpray's* cockpit, Calico purring in my lap, I watch a silvery crescent of new moon rise over the harbor and glance nervously up San Juan Channel toward that sparsely inhabited, darkly forested island where so many lives—my own included—were forever rearranged.

It all began when Zelda Jones, my red-haired part-time investigative assistant, dropped a Serenity and Light brochure on my desk with the suggestion that I sign up for the yoga retreat she was arranging for her newest client. In addition to providing esoteric computer research for my more obtuse cases, Zelda is a graphic artist and also does occasional events arranging. In this instance, her client was Mimi Rossellini, owner of the Hotel Dei Fiori on Santa Maria, who, desperate to improve her cash flow, had hired Zelda to organize and manage the retreat.

The Dei Fiori was formerly a convent that housed a dozen or so Franciscan nuns. The sisters raised grapes, made wine, and grew organic vegetables, which they sold at the Saturday Market in Friday Harbor. Over the years the number of novitiates had grown smaller and the nuns older until finally the convent was closed and the three-hundred-acre property was put up for sale.

The Serenity and Light brochure promised a cornucopia of delights: tranquility and wildflowers, meditation and *pranayama*, therapeutic massage and five-star Italian cuisine. The last was to be provided by Chef Piero, Mimi's new husband.

Although the price of the retreat exceeded my usual monthly living expenses, and a previous encounter with Bickram yoga had been less than harmonious, I could think of three reasons why I should treat myself to a luxurious sojourn at the Dei Fiori. One, the San Juan winter had been long, dark and wet, as winters in the far reaches of the Pacific Northwest often are. Two, as a result of the recent settlement of an insurance fraud case, my savings account sported a hefty balance. And three, Nicholas Anastazi, a Seattle maritime attorney and my significant other of almost ten years, would be occupied with his daughter Nicole's wedding during the week of the retreat. The wedding was to be held at the posh Rainier Club in Seattle, and my name was not on Nicole's guest list.

I felt bad about that. Very bad.

My body and spirit needed sunshine and wildflowers and all those other sybaritic delights.

So I said to myself, *Self, why the hell not?* and handed over my deposit.

Now, three months later, seated at the wooden refectory table in the second-floor dining room of the Dei Fiori, I contemplated the solitary orange, two squares of baked oatmeal, and small white cup of espresso that constituted breakfast, henceforth to be known as *prima collazione*. When Mimi Rosselini had fled to Italy after a messy divorce, she spent a month at a convent in Umbria before moving on to a friend's villa in Tuscany, where she wholeheartedly embraced Italian culture, including the language. Ergo, our retreat staff was ostensibly required to be conversant in Italian. I say ostensibly since I knew that Zelda's knowledge of Italian was limited to some choice lyrics from Italian opera. Last night's check-in was *ricezione*. After the evening repast—*la cena*—Mimi herded us across the cobblestone courtyard to Il Refugio for *círculo*, the evening "sharing circle" that reminded me of my daughter Melissa's long-ago kindergarten show-and-tell experiences. I am not a share-my-feelings person; my self-introduction was limited to my name and the fact that I lived in Friday Harbor aboard a thirty-eight-foot sailboat. On the way back to the hotel, Zelda told me that Mimi had wanted to end each day of the retreat with vespers, but Zelda had persuaded her to settle for something more secular.

I studied my horoscope for the day, tucked next to my plate—"fiery Aries should avoid confrontation and focus on peacemaking"—and turned to the printed agenda for Day One. Retreat participants would observe *prima collazione ne silenzio*, breakfast in silence. I bit into the baked oatmeal, so far unimpressed with *cucina italiana*, musing that the reason people lost weight at spas and retreats was probably that the food was inedible.

Natasha, the statuesque Russian woman with long chestnut hair who translated American romance novels into Russian, was a retreat participant as well as our resident massage therapist. She'd acquired her dual role—and had her registration fee waived—when the original therapist had canceled two weeks earlier and Zelda had noticed Natasha's previous experience in the "Comments" section of the registration form. Natasha was seated at the far end of the table on my left, next to two women from California who were wearing matching chartreuse leotards. They had introduced themselves at *círculo*: Danielle, fifty-something, tall, Semitic, dark-haired; and her roommate Zoe, a petite, perky blonde, probably in her late thirties. Zoe couldn't have weighed more than a hundred pounds. She was a talk-show host for a Santa Barbara TV station, but I hadn't a clue as to what Danielle did for a living or the nature of the relationship between the two women. They were billeted next to me in the recently renovated west corridor of the hotel.

Across from Zoe sat a trim, brown-skinned woman with shoulder-length, shiny dark brown hair. She wore a faded coral-colored cotton shirt over a black unitard. Although she was tall, around five foot eight, judging from the black eyes and the tawny tone of her smooth skin I'd noticed when I saw her at check-in, I'd guessed she had Hispanic and/or indigenous genes somewhere in her family tree. My guess had been confirmed when she had introduced herself last night in Spanish-accented English as a social worker from Los Angeles. Now she sipped her espresso and checked out the other guests from beneath long dark lashes. A fortuitous combination of Bridget Fonda and Sandra Bullock, she was named Andrea. Last night at *círculo* I'd noticed a green tattooed snake circling her left ankle. I found it hard to guess her age—thirty? thirty-five?—but judging from the firmness of her gluteus maximus and her triceps, I guessed she had access to a good fitness club. She felt my gaze on her, met my eyes, and smiled.

I glanced at the big clock on the stone wall. It was 8:32. I changed positions in my chair. My lower back was stiff from struggling to lower the mainsail in the rain and twenty-five knots of wind I'd encountered on my sail on *DragonSpray* from Friday Harbor the day before. I hadn't planned to sail to Santa Maria, but I'd cut the time short and had only ten minutes to lock up *DragonSpray* and walk from Slip G-73 at the Port of Friday Harbor marina over to the ferry dock when my cell phone rang. I recognized Nick's caller ID number. I answered it, praying Nicole had had a change of heart and he was calling to say I'd been invited to the wedding after all.

"Scotia. Glad I found you. Aren't you working today?"

"I'm headed over to Santa Maria. The yoga retreat, remember?"

"Sorry, I forgot. I'm going in circles."

"How are wedding preparations proceeding?"

"Nicole says there's a problem with the prenuptial agreement."

"What kind of problem?" I glanced across the water toward the green-and-white *Hiyu*. The last two cars were snaking into the mouth of the vessel. On the afterdeck, a tall, dark-haired figure in a windbreaker was speaking into a cell phone.

"Her fiancé doesn't want to sign it," Nick said.

"I see."

There were two or three seconds of dead air be-

tween us, then he asked, "Scotia, are you still upset
with me because you weren't invited to the
wedding?"

Upset, no. I was livid. Furious. Seething. "I'm
sure Nicole had her reasons."

"And I explained them to you. How awkward it
would be having you there with her mother."

"You two were divorced ten years ago, Nick."

"It's Nicole's wedding, Scotia. I couldn't force her
to invite you."

I glanced through the open companionway at the
ferry across the water and watched the last of the
cars disappear into the car deck. The tall figure in
the windbreaker was gone.

"I have to get on the ferry, Nick. There's not another one to Santa Maria until Saturday."

There was more dead air. "Nick, I have to hang
up."

"I'll call you later," he said abruptly. "Have a
good time at the retreat."

I hadn't made it on the ferry. I'd punched the End
button on the cell phone, resisted the temptation to
hurl it into the harbor, and sat in the cockpit seething with frustration and disappointment. Jaw
tightly clenched, I watched the ferry reverse out of
the slip, turn, and head out of the harbor into San
Juan Channel. Half an hour later, still angry, still
frustrated, I'd reluctantly gotten *DragonSpray* ready
to sail and headed up San Juan Channel, realizing
that I'd committed myself to the retreat for all the
wrong reasons.

I glanced again at the clock. 8:43.

To my left, Joseph Abbot, the tall, thin, ascetic

Serenity and Light yoga director, mindfully peeled his orange. Joseph was Mimi's brother, probably five years her junior, and, according to Zelda, a noted Sanskrit scholar. Next to Joseph was Tiffany Marr, a professional model with a passion for the color purple. Purple headband that controlled her mane of golden-blond hair, lavender cotton jumpsuit, iridescent mauve polish on her perfectly groomed fingers and toes. As my gaze lingered on the large, glittering, pear-shaped diamond on her third finger, left hand, she looked up from her oatmeal, met my eyes, then looked quickly away.

The chair on my right was empty. Last night Eric Szabo, a commercial photographer from San Francisco, had sat there. He'd never been to a yoga retreat and his enthusiasm for photographing the island's rugged topography had raised my dampened spirits. After *círculo*, we'd shared a cup of tea in the great room, chatted about his work and about my days as a security consultant in the city on the bay before I moved to Friday Harbor. Articulate, handsome, and courteous, Eric was the one person at the retreat I'd felt might be a kindred spirit. I missed him, and wondered if he'd decided to skip breakfast and get some early morning shots.

Beyond Eric's empty chair, Zelda Jones, her carrot-colored hair secured in a bouncy ponytail, was whispering behind her hand with Graham, the professor from Vancouver with blue-gray eyes and unruly, curly, dark gray hair. Graham was on sabbatical from the University of British Columbia to write a book about contemporary Latin American politics. His face was craggy and his eyes crinkled up when he smiled as he was doing now. At the far end of the table, Natasha whispered something to Zoe and Danielle frowned.

I gazed through the long narrow windows that overlooked the courtyard, where tall bushes of dark purple lilacs bloomed and the gardener was preparing terra-cotta pots for flats of red and white geraniums. The gardener's name was Gus. He was sixty-something, with a head of thick white hair and a well-trimmed white beard. According to Zelda, Gus had lived on Santa Maria for more than two decades. Mimi had introduced Gus and the rest of the staff—sexy, dark-haired Antonio, driver and all-around handyman; and Rita, the chambermaid—at *la cena* the previous evening. Rita's attitude left a good deal to be desired, and none of the three appeared particularly enchanted to see us. I pushed away the plate of baked oatmeal, which is one of two foods I most detest, took a sip of the espresso, and began to peel the orange, recalling the tidbits of history I'd gleaned from Zelda on the Dei Fiori and its innkeepers.

Mimi St. Clair, a San Francisco interior designer, had been divorced several years ago by her architect husband and replaced with a younger trophy wife. In Italy, after the cloistered month in Umbria, she attended cooking school and fell in love with an Italian chef. They were married three months later. Following a honeymoon in Sardinia, Mimi and Piero, accompanied by Piero's Aunt Serafina, returned to the West Coast, Mimi purchased the old convent on Santa Maria with her hard-won divorce settlement, and the couple set about converting it into a hotel.

When the renovation schedule lagged and she hit a cash-flow crunch, Joseph suggested a yoga retreat which he would direct. The participants could stay in the west wing of the hotel, where the renovation was most nearly complete, and Mimi had contracted with Zelda to advertise and organize the event.

I'd met Mimi when I checked in, a tallish, trim woman who seemed to favor long, flowing skirts. Her salt-and-pepper hair was close-cropped and her beautiful face had weathered at least fifty years. Piero had made an appearance at *círculo* last night. As I'd watched him fold his slender, medium-height frame onto a cushion beside Mimi with a dazzling smile on his olive-skinned face, I'd understood Mimi's enthusiasm for Italian *objets d'art*. Even if this *objet* was at least fifteen years her junior.

I returned to reading the day's agenda. Following *prima collazione,* there would be a break, then a two-hour yoga session with Joseph in Il Refugio. Lunch would be served from 12:00 to 1:00. A lecture and practice of *yoga mudra* were scheduled at 2:00. Massages could be booked with Natasha by signing the sheet on the bulletin board outside the dining room. *La cena* would be served at 6:00. *Círculo* would be held at 9:00.

I stole another look at the clock. One more minute of silence, then I intended to make a dash for the pay phone outside the dining room to check for voice messages. The Dei Fiori did not have phone lines in the guest rooms and cell phone service on the island was erratic at best. I finished the last section of the orange and rubbed my neck, which was stiff because I'd spent a good part of yesterday afternoon checking the trim of the sails and watching the windvane on the top of *DragonSpray*'s mast. The trip had been wet and uncomfortable, northwest up San Juan Channel almost directly into the teeth of the wind. I'd barely made it to the Dei Fiori dock before the late spring storm hit with a vengeance. All my muscles ached and I intended to book a massage. After which I wanted to meander up the hill to the meadow of wildflowers. The Butterfly Meadow, the brochure called it.

The previous evening, at Mimi's request, Zelda had kept us after dinner to review the "etiquette" of the retreat: *silenzio* would be observed for the first thirty minutes of breakfast and lunch. Outside guests were prohibited, as were smoking and alcohol. Incoming phone messages would be posted on the message board, where we could also leave messages for each other. Because there were no phone lines coming into Santa Maria, the hotel had installed several three-watt cell phones that mysteriously worked off of a tall antenna and provided service for the two offices and one public phone. There was no cable service to the island, but TV programs were available courtesy of a satellite dish.

I had no quarrel with the *silenzio* dictum since I'm not fond of making early morning small talk with strangers; actually, I'm not fond of making small talk at any time. I didn't expect any outside guests. I don't smoke and I could survive without my afternoon vermouth-and-soda ritual. However, the phone message plan annoyed me. For better or worse, I'm not one of those people who can go on vacation and blithely cut all ties to business, friends, and family. I have a high need to be connected. The large black hand on the clock crept past the number twelve. Silently, I slid my chair away from the table and scampered across the wooden plank floor. I had almost made it through the French doors leading to the hallway when I heard the tinkle of a small bell and heard Mimi's dulcet tones.

"Scotia, I have a short *annuncio*. Would it be possible . . . ?"

Feigning deafness, I opened the door and slipped into the hall, pulling the door shut behind me. I glanced at the message board. There were messages for Tiffany, Andrea, and Zelda, each one folded in half so that only the name of the guest was visible. Inside the antiquated wooden phone booth with its glass folding door, I perched on the round seat, dialed up my voice mail, and retrieved three messages. One from a new client who wanted me to find her biological mother; two from my daughter, Melissa, both of which contained a note of agitation. I dialed Melissa's number at St. Mary's College in the San Francisco Bay Area. She answered immediately.

"Mummy, you'll never guess who called me!"

The names of two of her departed boyfriends came immediately to mind, but I let sleeping dogs lie. "I give up."

"My father!"

Her father!? I blinked, speechless. Melissa had not

heard from her father for eighteen years. No birthday cards, no Christmas cards, no telephone calls. Simon Butler, my first husband, tall and lean with golden-brown eyes, had left us when Melissa was five. I was a senior at San Francisco State University when he departed on a scuba expedition to the Seychelles Islands in the Indian Ocean. The expedition was a graduation gift from his parents, and I had actually looked forward to having extra time to prepare for final exams and spend quality time with Melissa. The extra time had grown to several months, marked by one postcard a week. After six months, Simon took a job as a dive instructor and asked me for a divorce.

"*Mother*? Did you hear what I said? My *father* called me. He's back in Los Angeles. He wants to see me! He's flying to San Francisco and we're going to have dinner tomorrow night. Isn't that cool?"

"I heard you, Melissa." My brain felt like its neurons were encased in cold tar. "I'm sorry, I was just . . . surprised." Also shocked. Maybe even dismayed. Why now, after eighteen years of no contact with his only daughter? Or perhaps he had other children now. And a wife. "How did he find you?"

"Through Grandma. He tracked her down on the Internet and found her e-mail address."

"How do you feel about seeing him?" I asked stupidly.

"I'm a little . . . like nervous. Like except for the old pictures of him, I might not even recognize him."

"It's been eighteen years. I'm sure he's changed. Is he coming out to St. Mary's?"

"No, he doesn't have a car. I'm meeting him in the city tomorrow night. He's missed me and wants to get to know me. He says my grandma Butler would like to see me, too."

That he couldn't manage to rent a car and drive to the East Bay to see his daughter after eighteen years of silence was vintage Simon, but I said nothing. Through the window of the phone booth, I watched Danielle and Zoe, the two women in chartreuse leotards, exit the dining room, followed by Andrea, the woman from Los Angeles. Andrea glanced toward the phone booth, claimed her message from the board, read it, and glanced at the phone booth again.

"There's someone waiting for the phone, sweetie. Let me know how the dinner goes."

"I will, Mom. I had a hard time getting you. How come it took you so long to call back?"

I explained about the telephone system at the hotel.

"That's so lame. How can they run a hotel with no phones? Anyhow, I'll call you tomorrow night."

I hung up the phone, paralyzed by the thought of Simon appearing after eighteen years. I stared at the phone blankly, wondering what his sudden reappearance meant for Melissa, and slowly became aware of a tattoo of noise outside the phone booth. It was Andrea, foot tapping impatiently on the scarred oak floor. I hadn't returned the call to my client, but that would have to wait until my head was clearer. I opened the folding door and stepped out as Zelda came into the hall. Mimi followed her and the two women paused outside the French doors. Zelda was frowning. As I turned toward the stairway, I heard steps pounding up from the ground floor.

"*Il signore é morto! Lui é caduto! Il fotografo. Lui é morto.*"

The barrage of Italian came from Piero's Aunt Serafina. Face flushed, breathing hard, she grabbed at her long black cotton skirt, and stumbled on the top step. Her braid had come unplaited and her long, graying black hair swung around her face.

Mimi whirled around. "What do you mean, *signora*? What man is dead? What photographer?"

"*Il fotografo.* On the long step to the beach." Serafina touched her forehead. "He bleed."

"It's Eric," Zelda said quickly. "The photographer from San Francisco. He wasn't at breakfast. I *told* you those stairs to the beach were slippery. I'll call the EMS unit."

Mimi frowned. "But there was a chain across the steps. No one was supposed to go down there." She glanced down at the courtyard. "Perhaps we should wait until we find out . . ." Her voice trailed off.

"Call the EMS," I said, racing down the stairs.

2

I found Eric with one leg twisted under his body, lying at the very bottom of the narrow, extremely steep stone stairway that ended abruptly on a bluff above the waters of Boundary Pass. A length of rusty chain, apparently meant to serve as a gate, dangled from one side of the top railing. The narrow stone steps were wet from the recent storm. Many steps were cracked or broken. Even worse, halfway down, they were covered by a layer of spongy green moss, and the moss shifted when you stepped on it. Twice I nearly lost my footing and had to grab the wrought-iron railing for balance. Along the bottom third of the stairway, the railing had pulled completely away from the steps and lay on the hillside, supporting nothing. A small silver digital camera lay on the very bottom step.

Eric's handsome face was pale, his trim body motionless. Fearful of what I would discover, I knelt beside him and felt for the big carotid artery in his neck. To my relief, the pulse was there, but slow and weak. He lay partly on his stomach, his head lower than his feet, as if he had tripped and fallen headfirst.

"Is he . . . all right?" Mimi squatted on the step above me and peered at the unconscious man. Her face was nearly as white as the unfortunate photographer's.

"He's unconscious and he needs medical help immediately."

"Zelda called Friday Harbor for the EMS," Mimi said. "They're on their way. This railing was supposed to have been checked yesterday." Mimi turned and searched the apprehensive faces of the retreat participants clustered on the steps above her. "Has anyone seen Antonio?" she demanded.

There was no response, and I couldn't remember having seen the young handyman since dinner the night before. Mimi muttered something unintelligible and turned back to stare at the photographer's still face, with three reddish-blue bruises and a nasty cut that appeared to have stopped bleeding. "Should we carry him back to the hotel?" she asked.

"No," I said firmly. "We don't know the extent of his injuries. We need to wait for the EMS unit."

Although it is the county seat for San Juan County, Friday Harbor on San Juan Island does not have a hospital. However, the Emergency Medical Services unit includes a helicopter and medical technicians. They arrived by air eight minutes later, cleared the gawking guests from the stairway, and carried Eric's unconscious body up to the helicopter waiting in the driveway between the courtyard and the vineyard. Zelda had pulled Eric's registration and provided an emergency phone number for Eric's sister in Seattle. It was 10:34 when they lifted off, headed for the trauma center at St. Joseph's Hospital in Bellingham. Hands over my ears, I watched the bird rise straight up, bank to the north over the tall stands of Douglas firs that surrounded the hotel, then head due east under the heavily overcast sky.

"Lousy beginning for the retreat," Zelda said, carrying Eric's camera and preceding me through the heavy wooden door into the hotel's cavernous great room. "And unnecessary. I heard Mimi tell Antonio yesterday morning to put up a warning sign and make sure it stayed in place until the steps were cleaned off and the railing repaired. He's been less than cooperative since he got here."

"Where did she find him?"

"She posted a help wanted ad on a San Francisco Internet site. There were ten responses. The other nine evaporated when they found out about the two-days-a-week ferry schedule. Incidentally, the announcement you skipped out on this morning was that Joseph will be leading a meditation session at six A.M. every day in Il Refugio. He'll supply sitting cushions." She glanced at her watch. "I have to move Abigail to a room closer to the bathroom, but you could probably still make the Introduction to *Asanas* session."

Abigail Leedle, a colorful, retired high school biology teacher and wildlife photographer who was frequently embroiled in one or more political causes, was the only Friday Harbor participant besides myself.

I nodded. "I need to get out of these muddy shoes first. See you at lunch."

"*Collazione,*" Zelda corrected me with a grin, and headed for the stairway. I turned right through the archway and right again into the west corridor, nearly colliding with Piero and his aunt, who were standing just inside the dim passageway.

"*Lo ve lo ditto! Non fu un accidente.*" Serafina shook her head, hands on her hips.

I told you so. It wasn't an accident. Piero stood with his back to the archway and I paused, startled. My Italian is limited, but many words are close to Spanish, which I do understand.

"*Vieni, zia.*" Piero frowned, tucked his aunt's hand into the crook of his arm and drew her away toward the door to the library without noticing me.

I stared after the aunt and her nephew, then continued right into the corridor that ran the length of the west wing. I was on vacation and Eric's accident wasn't any of my business, nevertheless, I decided to take another look at where the railing had pulled away from the stairway before I headed over to Il Refugio.

The convent had been constructed in a U-shape around the large courtyard. I and the other the retreat participants—the hotel's only paying guests at the moment—were housed in the eight rooms of the west wing, four rooms on either side of the corridor. Serafina was billeted across the courtyard in the east wing with Mimi, Piero, Zelda, and the other three staff members.

The door to my room was darkly stained wood, thick and solid, and the large brass key turned easily in the old lock. I heard another key in the door behind me. I turned and nodded to Tiffany, the lavender-clad model. She returned the nod without smiling. The door closed behind her with a solid thud. Apparently I wasn't the only one who'd be late for *asanas*.

The only natural light in my room came from the high clerestory window on the east wall. I'd forgotten to turn off the small electric radiator when I went out to breakfast and the room felt stuffy. I stood on the step stool below the window and pushed it open a couple of inches. Living in a harbor aboard a boat has made me a bit of a fresh-air freak.

I took a dark blue parka from the closet, closed and locked the door, and pocketed the key. Mimi had said we needn't lock our rooms, but after working for twenty years in law enforcement and big-city security before moving to San Juan Island, I have only minimal trust in the human race. I pushed open the heavy exit door, with its wide horizontal lever that reminded me of the old doors at my high school in San Francisco, and stepped down into the courtyard. Gus had nearly finished planting the geraniums and didn't look up. Hands in the pockets of my parka, I paused, watching him tamp the dark soil around the last red-budded plant.

"Gus, did you happen to see Eric, the photographer, go out this morning?" I asked.

He stood up stiffly and brushed the soil from his faded blue jeans. He was taller than I had realized, at least six feet, and had bright navy blue eyes beneath thick white brows. "There were four guests out early this morning, ma'am. Three women and a man. The man was the one who had the accident."

"Were they together?"

"No. The man came out first and went off toward the beach." He gestured toward the stairway where Serafina had found Eric. "Then two women came out."

"What did the two women look like?"

"One was short and blond. Wearing green pants. Tight ones. The other one was the Russky."

The blonde would have been Zoe. I recalled that she and Danielle wore chartreuse leotards at breakfast.

"Did you see where they went?"

"They asked me how to get to the Butterfly Meadow."

"Do you remember how long they were gone?"

"About an hour, I'd say."

"What about the third woman?"

"She was the pretty one, the model." A small smile played around his mouth. "She was going to go to the beach, I guess, then it started raining and she came back."

I thanked Gus and cut across the courtyard to the path that meandered through the thick growths of salal and Oregon grape and ended at the stairway above the beach. The bushes had recently been trimmed. Thick mist hovered in the air from the recent rain. I stood in the damp silence at the top of the stairs, where someone had refastened the rusty chain and attached a hand-lettered sign that warned, DANGER DO NOT USE. I surveyed the steep incline and grasped the wrought-iron handrail on my right, pulled hard on it. It looked like holes had been drilled in the steps long ago and the railing set in concrete. The railing moved in the stone but did not come out. I continued carefully down the stairs to where I'd found Eric. Someone had removed the fallen railing from the hillside. I could see nothing on the stairs or alongside them that suggested Eric hadn't simply slipped. Nothing to validate Serafina's fierce whisper that Eric's fall hadn't been an accident.

I shrugged, climbed back up the stairs in the brightening morning, and looked up to find Antonio standing at the top, red metal toolbox in hand. I hadn't seen Antonio smile since I'd arrived, and this morning was no exception. He stood somewhere around five feet nine, had a slight build, longish, curly blond, probably bleached, hair, a thin brown mustache, and at least a day's growth of brown beard. The gold chain around his neck, the partially unbuttoned brown cotton shirt, the black pants and black windbreaker, were the height of urban cool. Los Angeles cool or Miami cool.

"Good morning, Antonio," I said. He nodded curtly without replying, brushed past me and walked down the stairs. I stood at the top watching his progress, wondering if he felt any guilt for Eric's accident. When he'd picked me up at the dock the night before and driven me and my one overstuffed duffel bag up the hill, I'd been grateful for his silence and not having to make small talk. Now, puzzled by what had brought him so far from his urban milieu, I decided his silence was more sullen than taciturn. I shrugged and headed back to my room to grab my yoga mat and join the others for *asanas* in Il Refugio. I was on vacation. Antonio's attitude wasn't my problem.

Nothing in my previous experiences with yoga prepared me for the tranquility of Il Refugio when I slipped through the side door about eleven fifteen. The room was layered in the hushed tones of Japanese flute music drifting from wall speakers. Lemony sunshine radiated through the two walls of windows. Barefoot, wearing white drawstring pants and a loose white cotton shirt, Joseph sat cross-legged on a dark red cushion at the designated front of the circular room. His long brown hair was tied back in a ponytail; his feet were bare. My coparticipants—six, now that Eric was gone—were seated cross-legged on mats or cushions in two semicircles. Joseph nodded to me, indicated a space on the carpeted floor behind Tiffany in the second row. I slipped out of my shoes and left them with the others by the door, then padded around to spread my mat between Graham, the tall Vancouverite, and Abigail Leedle.

"*Advaita* is a Sanskrit word," Joseph continued. "It means 'not-two.' *Advaitayana* yoga embraces the belief that the universe is all consciousness and that everything and everyone is an expression of that consciousness. There is no separation between you and anything in the universe. *Advaitayana* includes various disciplines of yoga, including *asana, pranayama, mudra,* and *yoga nidra*. At this retreat we will explore *asanas, pranayama,* and the *mudras*. Because today's session is shorter than I expected, I'd like to do a series of *asanas* called *surya-namaskar*, the sun salutation. I find it an excellent way to begin my day. I'll take you through each pose slowly and then we'll put it all together. After the sun salutation, I'd like to read you a bit from the thirteenth-century poet Rumi and then do a ten-minute meditation for Eric's recovery." He stood up with one fluid motion. "Please stand up and face the east."

Tiffany and the two women in chartreuse unfolded themselves from their mats and stood in the front semicircle behind Joseph, who had turned to face the sunshine coming through the arched window. Behind them, to my left, Abigail Leedle took her time getting her body from a sitting to a standing posture. I could almost hear her joints creaking.

"Stand with both feet touching. Bring the hands together in the *namaste* position . . . Inhale . . . and raise the arms upward . . . Slowly bend backward, stretching the arms above the head. Return the hands to the *namaste* position."

I brought my hands together and followed Joseph through the twelve positions of the sun salutation, feeling the stress of the past two days start to drain away. I made a formidable effort not to think about Melissa's impending reunion with her father or my last abrasive conversation with Nick. Or Eric's accident.

Returning to the starting position, I brought my palms together over my heart once again, stood in silence with the rest of the class, then sat down on my mat. Joseph opened a large book with an illustrated dust jacket and began to read. His voice was low and soothing, and I made a supreme effort to ignore the pain in my right hip bone.

"Jasmine comes up where you sleep. You breathe in dirt, and it sails off like a kite . . ."

3

Except for Andrea, the tall Hispanic woman from California, I was the last one in the dining room for lunch. When I left Il Refugio, my cell phone log indicated a missed call from Angela Petersen, my best friend in Friday Harbor and a San Juan County sheriff's deputy. When I tried to return the call, there was no service, and after twenty minutes, I gave up trying to get access to the communal phone, which had been preempted by Zoe. Before going into the dining room, I checked the message board and found one from Melissa. All it said was, "Call me." There was nothing from Nick.

A large urn of mushroom soup and a green salad were laid out on the wooden sideboard. I lined up behind Graham, Andrea, and Natasha. Outside the swinging door to the kitchen, Mimi and Piero spoke in inaudible tones. It was a conversation that seemed not to please either of them. Mimi glanced around the room, pausing when her eyes found Natasha, then turned back to resume the whispered conversation. Piero listened, shook his head violently, then abruptly lunged through the door into the kitchen. Mimi took a deep breath, stared at the swinging door, and headed for the sideboard with a bright smile in place. I returned her smile, thinking how good her hair looked with the blue silk shirt she was wearing, then helped myself to the soup and salad and a glass of lemonade.

"Eric's still unconscious," Zelda whispered as I pulled up my chair. "I'll make an announcement later."

Across the table Tiffany stared at Zelda, spoon poised over her soup, started to say something, glanced in Mimi's direction, and closed her mouth. Danielle was seated beside Zoe on Zelda's right. Natasha took a seat beside Tiffany. She wore what is termed "extreme sportswear": skintight black pants and a black, cropped camisole that revealed a lot of creamy skin and rounded bosoms. I wondered if the camisole would be able to resist gravity should she attempt a headstand and decided that Natasha's idea of appropriate yoga attire must have come from a catalog.

I glanced around the silent room, realizing how little we all knew about each other. Two meals a day in silence might promote our spiritual growth, but it wasn't going to do much to inspire rapport among the guests. Or did it matter? Did I really care? I've been accused of being antisocial. Mostly, I think, because I've never been good at chitchat, all those little verbal rituals that some people, particularly women, seem to produce effortlessly. I talk when I have something to say, and outside of business hours, that's usually to one of my two close friends in Friday Harbor: Angela Petersen and Jared Saperstein, the publisher of the *Friday Gazette*. Or to Nick. My last conversation with him certainly hadn't been effortless. Idly I stirred the mushroom pieces in my soup and wondered what, if anything, I was going to do about Nick's refusal to include me in his family events.

A little before one o'clock, Andrea came in silently, got her lunch from the sideboard, and took an empty chair beside Zoe. Without thinking, I glanced over at Danielle, who was watching Andrea with a face that looked like a thunderstorm.

The tinkling bell signaled the end of the enforced silence. Zelda, bright-eyed and smiling, stood up. "Group, a couple of announcements, before you run off. First, Joseph will be giving a lecture on universal consciousness in Il Refugio at two o'clock. Next, the whirlpool has been repaired and should be up to temperature by this evening. Be sure to cover it after you use it."

"Excuse me, Zelda," Natasha said, two vertical creases between her thick eyebrows. "I think the virlpool is too cold. You could possibly make it warmer? I do not like cold water."

"The whirlpool will be kept at 104 degrees," Zelda said firmly and changed the subject. "I know you all want to know about Eric and I'll provide daily announcements as long as he's hospitalized." She paused, glanced at Mimi, and referred to the sheet of paper she was holding. "Unfortunately, I do not have good news. Eric was medevaced to St.

Joseph's Hospital in Bellingham. He is still unconscious, still in the Intensive Care Unit. He has a
broken leg, multiple contusions, and a concussion.
His sister in Seattle has been notified and will be
visiting him."

Zelda hesitated, looked uncomfortable, glanced at
Mimi who nodded her head vigorously, then continued. "Mimi would like me to remind you it is
important that you make an effort to attend all the
yoga sessions. You have all paid a good deal of
money and she wants you to get your money's
worth. It will also be . . ." She paused again.
". . . important that we dine together at every meal
and create an esprit de corps."

I repressed a smile. Zelda, free spirit that she was,
usually eschewed rules, regulations, and mandatory
attendance for anything. She had clearly been co-
erced into making the announcement. Mimi gazed
around the room with a beatific smile as Zelda
picked up her dishes and disappeared into the
kitchen. Joseph muttered something that I didn't
catch, shook his head, and followed Zelda.

Zelda had beaten me to the public phone and I
still had no cell phone service. I was getting antsy
about business messages and e-mail, so I retrieved
my laptop from my room and trudged back to the
hotel office with the intent of persuading whoever
was there to let me plug into the main hotel line
long enough to download messages. I knocked on
the partly open office door. Mimi was on the phone.
She held up two fingers, which I interpreted to
mean she would be done in two minutes. I briefly

scanned her face, noticing that she had exceptional skin, porcelain and nearly poreless, but the two vertical lines between her brows were deeper than they had been yesterday, and her lipstick had worn away.

A large wooden desk overwhelmed the small office. Stacks of file folders and design and culinary magazines covered the top of the desk and the two file cabinets. Judging from the muffled sound of rattling dishes, the door on the back wall led to the kitchen. I moved to the window that overlooked a back patio and saw Danielle and Zoe standing below. Danielle, her arms folded tightly against her chest, her short dark hair tousled by the wind, was staring at the vineyard on the green hillside that rose gently behind the hotel. Zoe had one arm draped around Danielle's shoulder and was talking animatedly. Danielle listened and kept shaking her head.

Mimi replaced the receiver in the cradle. "Eric's being transferred," she said with a sigh. I turned away from the window. "They think there may be brain damage. They're moving him to Harborview Medical Center in Seattle." She shook her head. "That idiot Antonio. If only he'd done what I told him when I told him to do it."

Harborview is the primary trauma center not only for the state of Washington but for the entire Pacific Northwest. Patients are referred from as far away as Alaska. "I'm really sorry, Mimi," I said. "For Eric and for you. I know how hard you've worked to get the hotel going and make the retreat a success."

"And she's done a wonderful job." It was Andrea, standing in the doorway. "Sorry to interrupt, Mimi, but I was wondering if you could give me a tour of the grounds and the hotel today. I've been thinking that this would be a swell place to have a retreat for our agency. And I'm very sorry about Eric, too. How is he? Did I hear you say he's being moved?"

Mimi nodded. "They're taking him to Harborview Medical, in Seattle. His sister lives there." She bit her lower lip and glanced at the calendar on her desk. "Andrea, let's get a cup of coffee in the dining room and talk about what you have in mind for your retreat, and I'll show you around. Then I've got to go and arbitrate a dispute between Natasha, who insists that her meals be vegan, and my husband, who's threatening to go back to Italy unless he can serve Scampi a la Rossellini. No rest for the wicked."

I asked if I could connect to the hotel line for half an hour or so to retrieve messages.

"Sure. Go ahead and use my desk. The Internet is pretty slow here. I'm sorry about the phone situation. We were supposed to have lines in all the rooms by now, including data ports, but we're caught between the phone company that's still calculating how many thousands of dollars they're going to charge us to bring the service here from Orcas Island and some of the locals who don't want *any* phone service on Santa Maria." She gave me a brave smile, followed Andrea into the hall, and closed the door.

As I waited to be connected to the Internet, I recalled that when Zelda had been arranging the retreat she'd mentioned the animosity that the conversion of the convent into a hotel had stirred up among the small population of back-to-the-earthers on Santa Maria, a contingent of recalcitrants that had unsuccessfully petitioned the board of county commissioners to prevent Mimi from obtaining a building permit. When they weren't successful going through official channels, a series of malicious pranks began: one of the locals refused to let a barge loaded with construction materials dock; a power boat belonging to a stone mason from Friday Harbor mysteriously came "untied" from a mooring buoy and was found drifting five miles away in Boundary Pass; a delivery of supplies and tools disappeared just hours after it arrived. Stuff that could drive you crazy and nothing the sheriff could get a handle on.

I had three new e-mail messages. The first two were spam and I deleted them unopened. The third message came from Friday Harbor attorney Carolyn Smith: *Scotia: Harrison's sister just called to say that she heard from her nephew who's been sailing with Harrison on* Ocean Dancer *from Vietnam to Gibraltar. He says his dad is planning to cross the Atlantic to Trinidad this summer. Harrison's sister is threatening to sue me if I can't expedite the estate distribution. Any new ideas?*

For countless months I'd been attempting to locate Harrison Petrovsky, a blue-water sailor from Seattle, in order to secure his signature on documents necessary to distribute his late mother's estate. I'd hired investigators in Australia and Singapore and each time, either by coincidence or intent, Harrison had managed to sail away before we could deliver the papers. I glanced out the window at the gray clouds that had obscured the sun during lunchtime, thought about Nick enjoying wedding festivities in Seattle without me, and was tempted to offer to meet *Ocean Dancer* in Trinidad myself. Instead, I sent off an e-mail request to my previous employer in San Francisco, H & W Security, asking if they could recommend a process server in Trinidad.

As I was about to log off, another message popped up into the Inbox. It was from falcon@interglobal.com. I opened it. *Fate will soon take me to latitude 47. Is a rendezvous possible?* The only signature was a brown falcon that fluttered across the bottom of the screen, soared through the text of the message, and disappeared. I smiled.

Falcon. Code name for Michael Farraday, the enigmatic, brown-eyed British MI6 agent I'd met last summer while working on a case involving a homicidal sweetheart-swindler. Messages from Falcon had drifted in across cyberspace throughout the winter. Sometimes suggesting, sometimes inviting, sometimes simply *there.* The invitations had included a kite-flying festival in Japan, a train ride through the Peruvian mountains to Cuzco, and a scuba adventure on the Great Barrier Reef. I'd responded to each, but never accepted.

How could I? I had Nick.

Nicholas Anastazi, a six-foot-four-inch, overachieving Seattle maritime attorney I'd known for almost a decade. Gourmet cook, pianist, lover par excellence. Owner of a penthouse condominium overlooking Seattle's Elliot Bay and the Olympic Mountains. For almost a decade, those attributes were sufficient as long as I didn't dwell on the fact that I was only a peripheral part of Nick's life.

The weekend and occasional exotic vacation part.

Never included in holiday get-togethers with daughter Nicole, an art historian who lived in Seattle, or with his son, a dentist who lived in San Diego.

And most recently, not included in the wedding that would be taking place on Saturday.

At one time we'd had a brief conversation about our living together, but that was over a year ago. I stared vacantly at the computer monitor, attempting to analyze what it was about Nick that made me put up with behavior I wouldn't accept from any other man. And, as always, my analysis came back to one thing: chemistry. Or I thought it did. Would the chemistry still be there if Nick weren't so goddamn handsome and charming? Was that why I let him get away with keeping me at arm's length? Was he, in fact, a beautiful trophy?

I blinked and watched the tiny falcon that had returned to perch expectantly at the side of the e-mail window, and considered what I knew about the peripatetic agent Michael Farraday, with whom I'd helped to circumvent the U.S. justice system. Dark-haired, smart, clever, educated. Very fit, probably very virile. The passport I'd seen had shown a London address. And that's all I knew about him. I didn't know if he was married or had been. Didn't know if there was a "bird" waiting for him when he returned to London. Didn't even know if Farraday was his real name.

What do you have in mind? I stared at the words my fingers typed, then dispatched my reply, and the falcon went winging back . . . to where? Paris? Bangkok? Teheran?

I disconnected the modem and zipped the laptop into its leather bag. As I stood up, a sheet of paper fell off Mimi's desk onto the floor and landed faceup. I picked it up and read the ominous message: YOUR DAYS ARE NUMBERED. GET THE HELL OFF THE ISLAND OR SOMETHING WORSE WILL HAPPEN. The small block letters were printed in black ink. I read it again, then replaced the letter on the desk, wondering if it had arrived before or after Eric's accident. The phone rang, rang again. I hesitated, then answered it. "Hotel Dei Fiori."

"I would like to speak to Ms. Tiffany Marr." The caller was male and spoke with a Spanish accent.

"I'll be happy to give Ms. Marr a message," I said.

"Tell her to call Roberto immediately."

"Is there a phone number?" I inquired dutifully.

"She knows it." He hung up.

I scribbled out a message on a pink slip, tacked it up next to the other one for the blond model, and put my name down for a massage at 4:00. It was 2:14. A little late to show up for the lecture on universal consciousness. Just time for a nice nap before my massage.

The freshening breeze that swept the courtyard smelled of lilacs and the ocean. The gray clouds had become high, white cumulonimbus. A rectangular window of blue sky was forming, a sign of a high-pressure area lying offshore and of strong winds within the next ten or twelve hours. A hand waved at me from near the outside entrance to the west wing. It was Graham, the geology professor from Vancouver, ensconced in one of the freshly painted red Adirondack chairs. He was working on a silver laptop that looked a good deal more state-of-the-art than mine.

"Lovely afternoon, Scotia. I see you also missed the lecture."

"I had some catching up to do," I said guiltily. "How's the book going?"

"Page by page. I write five pages a day, no matter how bad it is. Amazing how it adds up."

"Does the book have a title?"

"*The Politics of Oil in the Western Hemisphere.*"

He gestured to the other red chair, "Would you like to sit down?" A large, gray cat was curled underneath. I recalled that the cat's name was Mao.

"I thought the Middle East was where all the oil politics were happening," I said, sliding into the chair. "Though now that you mention it, wasn't there a coup in Venezuela last year? Wasn't that about oil?"

"There was an *attempted* coup, and I happened to be down there at the time, researching the book. The strike at PDVSA by the management triggered the president's strong-arm tactics. It was the last straw in almost a decade of increasing authoritarian tactics by the president. Eight hundred thousand people took to the streets in total outrage, demanding that he leave office immediately. The coup was put down and the instigators left the country. That is, the ones who didn't end up dead."

"What's PDV . . . what did you call it?"

"PDVSA. Petróleos de Venezuela, S.A. It's the state-owned oil industry that furnishes around 13% of U.S. oil. They're the fifth largest producer in the world."

"I didn't know it was that much. Your Spanish is excellent. Where did you learn it?" I asked, rearranging myself in the chair as Mao jumped into my lap.

"I was born in Caracas. Lived there till I was fourteen. My father worked for Chevron, and my sister's still there."

"Have the politics stabilized there since the attempted coup?" I asked, watching Abigail charge across the courtyard with her large rucksack.

He shook his head. "The situation's deteriorating."

"In oil or in politics?"

"In Caracas, they're one and the same. Just now there's a move afoot for a referendum to recall the president, who's trying to go after foreign investment into the oil industry. And a lot of Venezuelans are opposed to that."

"Is that something Washington would like to see happen?"

"Anything that gives the U.S. companies greater access to Venezuelan oil reduces the dependency on Middle Eastern oil."

"And that would happen sooner rather than later, if the U.S. automakers would get off their duffs and design fuel-efficient cars!" Abigail chimed in, pausing beside my chair.

"You're eighty percent right, Abigail," Graham said. "But most of my Canadian friends don't think that's going to happen anytime soon. They believe that Americans are wedded to big cars and that the automobile industry wants to keep the consumers happy and that the government needs campaign funds from the automakers and . . ."

". . . and so we remain enslaved by Middle Eastern oil," Abigail finished for him, gathering up her rucksack. "See you two at dinner, or whatever it's called." She trotted off toward the main entrance and Mao leaped from my lap to follow her.

"Tell me about Venezuela," I said. "Could we actually import enough oil from there to replace our dependence on the Middle East?"

"Not at the present rate of consumption. Besides, I don't think Venezuelan politics will stabilize anytime in this decade. The World Bank has frozen loans, and terrorism is growing by the day. Political terrorism and terrorism specific to the oil industry. There is a small group of Venezuelan exiles living in the U.S., most of them in Southern California, who are trying to engineer a change of presidency. They're getting closer." He shut the laptop and stood up. "I didn't mean to bore you. You probably came here for peace and quiet."

I glanced at my watch and stood up. "It's not boring, but I would like to get a nap in before my massage appointment."

My room was the first one on the right from the courtyard entrance. Zoe and Danielle's was next, then Eric's. Graham's was the last one on the right next to the "W.C." He left me at my door with an engaging smile and a salute. Across the hallway, Tiffany's door stood partly open and she was standing in the open door of Natasha's room, which was across from Zoe and Danny's. My room was no longer stuffy and the wind blowing through the open window had turned cool. I was about to close the window when I heard sharp voices from the room next door.

"It's a personal issue, Zoe. You know that."

"It's about conscience and ethics, Danny. Nothing more, nothing less. You're making a mountain out of a molehill and I'm losing patience. We've had this conversation before. Let's get on with it."

"Conscience and ethics *are* personal, Zoe. Neither of my daughters has talked to me since the divorce. I tried to tell you that. I'm not ready. I still . . . still can't believe what you did to poor . . . Jeremy." Danny's voice broke and I heard her sobbing.

Soberly I pulled the clerestory window shut, latched it, and drew the oyster-colored drape over it. Unless it has something to do with an investigation, I abhor eavesdropping. I didn't want to know what Danny wasn't ready for or what Zoe had done to Jeremy, whoever he was. There appeared to be a conflict between the two women in the adjoining room, which would explain the tension I'd picked up between them since they'd arrived.

Yawning, I set the alarm clock for three forty-five, folded back the white damask bedspread, removed my shoes and yoga pants, and slid between the sheets. I missed my own pillow, missed Calico, the furry feline I shared with a dockmate back in Friday Harbor, missed *DragonSpray*'s rocking against her lines. Just before sleep overtook me, I remembered that I should hike down to the dock to check *DragonSpray*'s mooring lines after my massage.

4

The massage studio, a two-room stone cottage located adjacent to Il Refugio in a grove of madrona trees, was dim and aromatic with oil of lavender, the sheets on the massage table soft and white. A wood fire burned in the small freestanding corner fireplace. Natasha had magic hands: my shoulders were kneaded and acupressured, my neck and spine stretched, my gluteus maximus and related muscles reduced to the consistency of soft bread dough. I drifted in and out of a light sleep, wondering why Nick hadn't called. Wondering what, if anything, I could do about the holes in our relationship. Fragments of the conflicted interchange between Zoe and Danny floated through my brain, and I wondered if I should talk to Mimi about the paper I'd seen with its ominous threat. It was five o'clock when Natasha finished, five fifteen by the time I roused myself to dress, which left me less than an hour to hike down to the dock to check *DragonSpray*'s lines before *la cena*.

Whether by coincidence or because he was lying

in wait for me, I found Graham sitting on a bench outside Il Refugio and he asked if he could tag along. The sky was blue now, with high, white clouds and a cool, brisk wind. The one-lane road meandered through a grassy meadow and then descended a gentle slope to the rickety wooden ramp above Santa Maria Harbor.

"I'm mostly an armchair sailor, Scotia," Graham confessed, as we paused at the landing overlooking the small bay. "My fantasy is to live in a place like this with a sailboat tied up to my dock." He gave me an infectious grin. "Zelda says you're a live-aboard. Are you a blue-water sailor?"

"Mostly coastal cruising. San Diego, the west coast of Mexico, San Francisco. And I've done some cruises up here." Weekend cruises with Nick to the Gulf Islands or over to Victoria at the tip of the Sechelt Peninsula. A four-week cruise north of Desolation Sound before he became one of Seattle's most successful admiralty lawyers.

We headed down the ramp to the marina and I noticed that *DragonSpray*'s bow was floating farther away from the dock than the stern was. And that a man was doing something with her mooring lines. I flashed on what Zelda had told me about the stonemason's boat that had "come untied" and been found floating in Boundary Pass.

"Do you single-hand?" Graham asked.

"Sometimes," I answered absentmindedly, quickening my pace, wondering if I'd been so tired and distracted after yesterday's sail that I hadn't properly tied the lines.

"This your boat?" The man was bearded, with

thick, dark brown hair, a green-and-black plaid wool shirt, thick work boots.

"Yes, it is. What's the problem?"

"The bow line came loose. I replaced it." He glanced over his shoulder toward the mouth of the harbor, seemed about to add something, then changed his mind. He handed me the old bow line. "Looks like it frayed out. Might be a good idea to put a non-chafe protector on it. And the spring line was loose. I retied it."

"It *had* a non-chafe protector on it," I snapped, staring at the frayed line. "And the spring line was properly tied yesterday."

He shrugged and stood up. "Just trying to help, ma'am. That was quite a storm last night."

"Do you live here?" I asked sharply, recalling Zelda's comments about the difficulties the locals had given Mimi.

"Yes, ma'am. I live here, my daddy lived here, my granddaddy lived here."

"Who are you?" I demanded, realizing as I said it how rude I must have sounded.

"John Jordan." He gave me an appraising look, glanced at Graham, and reluctantly extended his hand. I shook it, feeling the hard calluses and the muscular fingers.

"I'm sorry," I said. "I'm Scotia MacKinnon. This is Graham Bartlett. We're staying at the hotel."

"Pleased to meet you." He produced a one-sided smile. "Before you ask what I'm doing on the hotel's private dock, I was headed up to the hotel to see a woman. Her name's Natasha. She's from Russia."

"But . . ." I glanced at Graham, recalling Mimi's prohibition against outside guests.

Graham shook John's hand and smiled ruefully. "If your lady friend is at the same retreat we're at, outside guests aren't allowed."

Jordan frowned and shook his head. "I pay for her ticket all the way from Moscow to Seattle and you tell me I can't see her? I don't think so." He walked briskly up the dock, climbed the canted ramp, and disappeared over the top of the hill.

I stared after him, realizing that our bosomy translator-cum-massage therapist had had more on her Russian mind than *asanas* when she'd signed up for the retreat.

I examined the frayed line John Jordan had handed me. I knew for certain I had tied the lines properly yesterday.

"I heard a rumor that our innkeeper didn't exactly receive a royal welcome from her neighbors when she moved in," Graham commented thoughtfully. "You think there's more to Mr. Jordan than meets the eye?"

"Maybe," I said, still staring at the frayed line. "Maybe not."

5

People go on retreats in Bali and in Costa Rica and on California's Big Sur coast, in the north of Scotland and the outback of Australia. They travel alone to find solitude or in hopes of finding a significant other. They go away in pairs to get reacquainted. They arrive in groups to celebrate an anniversary or create corporate esprit de corps. The expectations are to lose weight or learn to meditate, to acquire a brighter, clearer complexion, or to improve one's tennis serve.

In theory, the eight retreat participants at Serenity and Light had signed on with the expectation of learning yoga or improving their practice. As I would discover fairly soon, the agenda for each of my fellow retreat participants was more complex than that. When the participants' agendas did not correspond to the agenda of the retreat, life became interesting, as it was just now inside the French doors to the dining room when Graham and I arrived for dinner.

"I came to Serenity and Light to find American husband." Natasha, hands on her hips, dressed for dinner in a garnet sweater, long black skirt, and black high-heeled boots, was addressing Mimi, who was attempting to block the doorway. "I meet them on the Internet. They are romantic, like in the books that I translate. They luf me. But only one sent me a ticket. I have a right to see this man. Besides, I am doing you a favor to do massages."

"Natasha, I appreciate your doing the massages. But it is important to the retreat *process* that we share the sessions and the meals together and that we not allow outside guests to interrupt our bonding."

"I don't care an elephant's toenail about your *process* or your *bonding*," Natasha said, shouldering her way around our distressed innkeeper. "What are you going to do? Send me to Siberia?" Natasha's English grammar was nearly perfect; only her pronunciation and the Russian cadence to her sentences betrayed her origin.

Repressing a smile, I checked the message board, noticed that Tiffany had not picked up her message from Roberto, and found a folded pink slip with my name on it. It was from Angela Petersen. The communal phone booth was empty. I closed the folding glass door and dialed the sheriff's office, watching the staff and guests file into the dining room: Joseph, radiant in white pants and a white shirt; Zoe chatting with Abigail; Serafina, glowering and draped in black.

The sheriff's office answered on the first ring and I was transferred to Angela.

"Deputy Petersen."

"Angela, it's Scotia."

"You and Abigail still at the yoga retreat on Santa Maria?"

"I got here last night. Abby came over on the ferry. What's up?"

"We got an inquiry from the Seattle P.D. about an hour ago. They responded to a call at Harborview Medical. Some nut insisted he wanted to see a patient named Szabo. Assaulted a nurse in the I.C.U. and then took off before the security guys got there. Does that ring a bell?"

"*Eric* Szabo?"

"Yes. He was transferred to Harborview from St. Joseph's in Bellingham around one o'clock, after being medevaced to the mainland from a hotel on Santa Maria Island. There's only one hotel that I know of on Santa Maria, but I couldn't remember the name. I thought you might know something about Szabo."

"It's the Dei Fiori," I said, troubled by what Angela had told me. "Eric had an accident this morning. Slipped on a stone stairway. He was unconscious when the EMS took him away."

"What do you know about him?"

"Only that he's a commercial photographer from San Francisco."

"Anyone else there know him?"

"I have no idea. He has a sister in Seattle. You should probably talk to Mimi Rossellini, the hotel owner. I'll ask her to call you."

"Thanks. Give her my cell phone number. Seattle P.D. wants to know if there's any reason why they should put a guard on the guy. How are things otherwise? Isn't Nick's daughter getting married in a big ceremony this coming weekend?"

"Yes."

"That's all? Just 'yes'? Not, 'I'd like to kill the bastard for not inviting me'?"

"I'd like to kill the bastard for not inviting me and if I don't go in to dinner, I'm going to be *persona non grata* with the innkeeper, or whatever they call it in Italian."

"Ciao." She chuckled and cut the connection.

I hung up and left a note on the message board for Mimi to call Angela. Andrea was racing up the stairs as I left the phone booth. Zelda ushered the two of us into the dining room with a flourish and I wondered why she looked so smug. I took the empty chair at the end of the table, thinking about my conversation with Angela, pondering what a photographer from San Francisco might have done to provoke the break-in at the Intensive Care Unit.

Dinner that Wednesday evening was a huge antipasto platter of hearts of romaine with slices of tomato and fresh mozzarella drizzled with olive oil and served with warm, crisp bread, followed by spaghetti and meatballs. The repast would have been vastly improved with a glass of chianti, but it was far more inspiring than last evening's cheese sandwiches and split pea soup. Score one for Piero.

"You look preoccupied," Zelda said, spooning eggplant-and-pine-nut appetizer onto her bread.

"Eric was transferred to Seattle Harborview," I said. "A man tried to get into his room and assaulted one of the I.C.U. nurses when he wasn't allowed in."

She stared at me, bread halfway to her mouth. "Who was it?"

"Don't know." I related my conversation with Angela. "Is there anyone here who knows him?"

She chewed her bread thoughtfully. "Yeah. Tiffany does. I think she met him on a modeling assignment she did recently. But she sure didn't look happy to see him yesterday." She glanced down the table to where Tiffany was seated between Zoe and Abigail. There was no sign of Graham, or of Danielle, and I wondered if she and Zoe had resolved their differences.

"I left a note on the board for Mimi," I said, winding the spaghetti around my fork. "Angela wants to talk to her."

Zelda frowned. "What for?"

"The Seattle police want to know why someone tried to break in and if they need to post a guard outside Eric's room."

"I'll call Eric's sister. I talked to her right after he was medevaced out of here. Mimi's got enough on her mind. This afternoon she got the estimate from the phone company. They want fifty thousand dollars to bring in phone lines from Orcas. I don't know how she's going to afford it."

I finished the spaghetti and began on the salad. "Pity Mimi chose this island for the hotel," I said. "No electricity, no phones, no daily ferry, unfriendly locals."

"She looked at properties on San Juan and Orcas. She couldn't afford them. This was cheaper, since there's only two ferries a week. Besides, she fell in love with this place. It reminds her of the little convent in Umbria where she spent a month after her divorce. Gus promised to help her replant the vineyard. I think she'll make it if she can just hang on for another two or three months until the renovations are done."

I was about to point out that in another three months it would be August, and the tourist season in the San Juans dwindles sharply after Labor Day, when the swinging door to the kitchen opened and Piero brought in a tray. "There's zabaglione for dessert," Zelda said. "Shall I bring you one?"

I nodded, watching Mimi's handsome husband unload small glass dessert dishes from the tray. In the corner by the window, Serafina sat in silence across the table from her nephew's wife. Mimi, brows knitted, leaned toward Antonio, who was staring sullenly at his plate.

He stood up suddenly. "Okay, so I forgot," he burst out. "I can't remember everything." He gathered up his dishes and pushed his way through the swinging door into the kitchen. I wondered if his forgetfulness had to do with not repairing the stairway where Eric had fallen or if some new omission had occurred.

Zelda returned to the table with the zabaglione and a small plate of macaroons. "I'm going to talk to Mimi and then I have to track down a big order of stuff for the hotel that was supposedly delivered to the post office and then got returned. Rugs and pillows and stuff. See you later." She tucked two macaroons into her zabaglione and headed for Mimi's table.

Spooning up the velvety gold dessert with its subtle flavor of anisette, I stared through the window overlooking the courtyard. The wind was still blowing and the courtyard was bright with sun. Suddenly I wanted to get away from the petty conflicts among the guests and our innkeeper's problems with her neighbors and take a long walk. Mimi was deep in conversation with a scowling Serafina. I decided to make a run for freedom before she noticed me subverting the retreat process.

The path behind the hotel skirted the old vineyard and then climbed steeply for half a mile. Hands in my pockets, head down, I followed the trail through tall green grasses and bushes of pink Nootka roses thinking about the challenges Mimi was facing: abandoned by her husband for a trophy wife. Married to a man at least fifteen years her junior. A ghoulish aunt. Trying to turn a dilapidated old convent on a remote island into a cash-producing enterprise. It was overwhelming, even without the dirty tricks the locals were playing on her or Eric's unfortunate accident. As I climbed the last ten yards of the hill, the throaty notes of a flute drifted down from the meadow, more a tonal contemplation than a song, and as I climbed over the crest of the hill I discovered the flautist. It was Graham, back against a large rock facing out toward Boundary Pass, blowing into a long bamboo flute.

I stood looking west across the carpet of wildflowers and beyond to the white-capped waters that separated the U.S. from Canada. To the uninitiated, the islands of the San Juan Archipelago are big piles of rocks, thickly forested with tall stands of Douglas firs, surrounded by menacing dark blue waters. In reality, many of the islands consist of rolling meadows and grass-covered prairies that blossom into a kaleidoscope of wildflowers in spring and summer.

Santa Maria Island is shaped like a boomerang with the inverted "U" facing to the southeast. The Hotel Dei Fiori nestles on a hillside above a small valley. Above the hotel lies a crest of mountains overlooking Boundary Pass to the west and the protected waters of Santa Maria Sound to the south.

The island is not for the pampered urban dweller. According to the most recent census, it has a population of eighty-four. It has a small school and mom-and-pop grocery, but no restaurant, no bar, no fitness club. A two-lane dirt road follows the perimeter of the island from the southwest to the northeast. Water comes from private wells and power is supplied by private gasoline or diesel generators. As I'd already discovered, cell phone reception on the island is "geographically challenged." In all respects, Santa Maria Island is "off the grid" and happy to be so.

The flute went silent, the last notes seeming to float gently away on the wind. Graham turned and stood up. "Spectacular, isn't it?"

I nodded. "Both the scenery and the music. What kind of a flute is that?"

"It's called a *shakuhachi*. Part of the seven-hundred-year-old Japanese tradition of 'blowing

Zen.' They were used for centuries by traveling monks called *komuso*. I was fortunate to be taught by one of my professors in graduate school who'd lived in Japan. How was dinner?"

"Uneventful except for an improvement in the cuisine. I needed to get some fresh air and wanted to see the meadow. Unfortunately, I can never remember the names of the flowers."

"Sheep sorrel and Western buttercup," he said. "Some Menzies larkspur. Chocolate lilies. And the little guys are Tomcat clover." Graham squatted down and fingered the diminutive clover. "The butterflies are Spring Azures and Silvery Blues. Gus told me the locals call this the Butterfly Meadow."

"I thought you were a political scientist." I sat down on a rock outcropping in the midst of the multicolored carpet of blooms and watched the flutter of lavender butterflies hovering over the blossoms. "How did you learn about flowers?"

"I was a high school botany teacher before I found my true calling. At a one-room school over on Vancouver Island." Graham found a large flat rock next to mine. "And has private investigation always been your true calling? Did you grow up wanting to be a female Sam Spade?"

I didn't remember telling anyone at the retreat how I earned my daily bread, but Zelda probably had. Discretion is not one of her virtues. I shook my head. "I grew up wanting to be a librarian like my grandmother."

He chuckled. "What happened?"

What had happened had to do with the man I had married when I was nineteen, the very Simon

Butler who was about to visit our daughter for the first time since she was five. "I got distracted," I said lightly. "Got a degree in criminal psychology, went to the Police Academy, ended up a domestic-relations detective for the San Diego P.D., followed by private security work in San Francisco." A thumbnail sketch of twenty years of single parenting and the mean streets of law enforcement, one divorce and two dead husbands, broken promises and broken dreams.

"You're a California native? I wouldn't have guessed," Graham said.

"I was born on Cape Breton Island, Nova Scotia. Daughter of a fisherman and a Boston flower child. After my father and grandfather died in a winter storm off the Grand Banks, I ended up in San Francisco with my mother and her Italian lover when I was thirteen."

I stood up. Whatever emotion registered on my face must have indicated that my childhood was not something I wanted to talk about.

"I'm sorry." Graham got to his feet and carefully put the flute in a long canvas rucksack. "Sorry about your father and sorry that I was prying." He put the rucksack on his shoulders and glanced at the trail that led to the other side of the meadow. "Gus says there's a spectacular view from the top of that crest, and a valley beyond. Want to do some exploring? Or did you want to get back for *círculo?*"

"*Círculo* can do without me. Let's explore."

I followed Graham's long legs across the meadow, around three huge granite boulders, probably deposited ten thousand years ago by the retreating Vashon glacier, and up a crest that left me breathless by the time we reached the summit.

We followed the bluff-top trail along the rocky coast for a mile or so, then turned inland. Half a mile further on was another meadow, overlooking a small, deep valley with three dwellings. Smoke ascended from the chimney of what looked more like an old two-storey stone stable than a house. From inside the stable a dog barked; the deep, hearty bark of a large dog. In the corral attached to the stable, a large, dark horse, almost black, was munching on a pile of hay. When the dog barked, the horse lifted his head, sniffed the air, and went back to his dinner. A cluster of white beehives occupied a small green meadow in front of the stable.

"This must be where Gus lives," Graham said. "He's a beekeeper as well as a gardener. I talked to him yesterday when he was working in the garden. He moved up here from somewhere on the Olympic Peninsula when his wife died twenty years ago."

"What has he done here all this time?"

"He was the gardener and handyman at the convent. I asked why the convent closed, but he didn't want to talk about it."

"The stories vary according to the teller," I said. "I believe the order started with twenty nuns, but it was so remote they had a hard time recruiting young novitiates. It closed about five years ago and the remaining sisters moved over to eastern Washington."

He frowned. "But I thought Mimi bought the convent from the estate of a woman from California."

I nodded. "She died," I said, not mentioning that

the woman from California who had bought the property intending to convert the convent into a winery and bed-and-breakfast had been murdered. Shot while out for a morning run, by the man who had married her and swindled her out of a lot of money. A man I'd eventually tracked down, a few days too late.

"Well, hopefully the current innkeepers will have better luck," Graham said.

"It's going to be a struggle."

"You mean all the pranks and dirty tricks?"

I nodded and told him about the threatening note I'd seen, but omitted any mention of the trouble at Harborview.

"I hope Mimi makes it," he said. "She seems really nice, and it's a wonderful use of the convent."

It was after ten and nearly dark by the time we scrambled back down the hill. Fortunately Graham had taken a flashlight. *Círculo* was over. Windows were lit in both the east and west wings of the hotel. I walked down our corridor to the great room, hoping the big bowl of fruit had been replenished. Abigail, wrapped in a faded pink chenille robe, was curled alone on the leather sofa by the fireplace eating a red apple and perusing the latest edition of the *Friday Gazette*. Her long white hair, usually contained in a thick braid, hung loose and silky around her shoulders. I picked a small cluster of purple grapes from the bowl and joined her on the sofa.

"You and Graham were chastised in absentia," she advised, folding the newspaper. "I hope you

enjoyed whatever you were doing with that attractive professor." She grinned and took another crisp
bite of the apple.

"The handsome professor and I hiked over to the
valley where the gardener lives. Aside from our ab-
sence, how was *círculo*?"

"Natasha didn't show. Zoe made some very
oblique comments about personal integrity that nobody understood except, apparently, Danielle, who
started crying and went off to her room. And I am
viewed as being uncooperative."

"You didn't share your feelings?"

"I said I came to the retreat to improve my body
and do some serious thinking, not to wash my dirty
laundry in public. And that some feelings are better
left unshared."

The tall wooden clock to the right of the stone
fireplace chimed twice. Ten thirty. I yawned, finished the grapes, stood up.

"You have a message on the board upstairs,"
Abby said, opening up the newspaper. "I think it's
from your sweetheart."

A message from Nick. Feeling like a teenager, I
raced up the stairs, found the message tacked up
beside two messages for Tiffany. The call-back number on the pink slip was Nick's cell phone. I slipped
into the phone booth, dialed his number, and listened in disappointment to his businesslike recorded voice. "This is Nick Anastazi. I'm either on
another call or out of range. Please leave your name,
number, and a message and I'll call you back."
Businesslike was not what I wanted from Nick at
the moment.

I sighed, left my name and the hotel number, and walked back to my room with a disconsolate heart. With minimal cell phone service and the hotel office locked, he wouldn't be able to reach me until the next morning. Even if he did call back. I turned on the electric radiator, took one of the big white monogrammed Dei Fioni towels from the hook beside the closet, grabbed my flannel pj's, robe and slippers, and trudged down the hall to the communal bath. Half an hour later, I was back in my room, hydrated, shampooed, and fragrant with wild raspberry body lotion. I crawled into bed, and fell asleep over *The Girl in the Plain Brown Wrapper*.

Sometime later I jerked awake, sweaty and cramped, with the book over my nose. Wondering what had awakened me, I peered into the corridor, saw Natasha's back disappear into her room, heard the door close and the lock click. I hoped she'd had a romantic evening with her Santa Maria suitor. I turned off the radiator, opened the window, and was about to climb back into bed when I heard voices drifting through the window from the room next door.

". . . you sure, Zoe?"

"Ninety-nine percent positive. Remember the story I was working on . . . year? The gang story? . . . tattoo is identical."

Danielle's pleading voice: "Zoe darling, this retreat was supposed to be a vacation for us. What about the suspension?"

". . . too big. And it's just what I need to . . ."

The voices faded to an unintelligible murmur. I thought about Danielle's "Zoe darling" and I decided it was possible the two women were more than just friends. On the remote chance that I'd feel like attending early morning meditation with Joseph, I wound my little Baby Ben and set it for 5:45. About to turn out the light, I saw a gray, furry shape leap onto the bed from the high window. It was Mao, Mimi's cat, who must have leaped to the high window from the fir tree outside. He crouched, sniffed my outstretched hand, walked across my stomach, and curled up beside my shoulder, purring loudly. The purring was comforting. I turned out the light, stroked Mao's silky head once or twice, and then was asleep.

6

On Thursday, the alarm awakened me at 5:45, whereupon I considered attending 6:00 A.M. meditation with Joseph for all of five seconds, and dozed off again to dream of two women in chartreuse arguing over a white wooden beehive. The small blond woman began to pound on the hive. Fearful that the pounding was going to make the bees unhappy, I moved toward her to warn her and woke to sharp knocking on my door. It was Zelda.

"Scotia? Wake up! I need to talk to you."

The hands on the Baby Ben pointed to 7:15. Breakfast wasn't until eight. What was the hurry? Mao had departed. Muted morning light seeped through the open window. The knocking resumed, louder and more urgent.

"Scotia? Are you awake?"

"I am now," I said in annoyance. "Hold on." I pushed back the thick comforter and shivered in the frigid air. With one foot on the cold stone floor, I found my slippers and groped in the closet for my flannel robe. I belted the robe and opened the door. Zelda was in pajamas, red flannel with a white embroidered crest over the pocket that said "Campfire Girls." Her long, carrot-colored hair was a rat's nest, her usual jocularity missing, her green eyes wide. Freckles stood out on her pale face. Behind her, Tiffany's door opened and the blond model watched us with puffy red eyes, arms hugging her chest over lavender satin pajamas.

"What's wrong?" I asked, nodding to Tiffany.

"It's Zoe Llewelyn, the TV woman." Zelda shivered, her voice husky. "She's dead."

"What?" I stared at her in shock, my sleepy brain struggling to process the information. Across the hall Tiffany gasped and closed her door. I motioned Zelda inside. "Did I just hear you say Zoe is dead?"

"Yes; she fell off the bluff at the Butterfly Meadow. Danielle is hysterical. Mimi wants to talk to you." She continued to shiver.

"Are you sure?" I glanced at the window, recalling fragments of the midnight conversation I'd overheard. "Where is she?"

"I *told* you. She fell from the cliff. Her body is on the rocks. Mimi's waiting for the sheriff." She curled up on my bed, still hugging her chest.

I wrapped the comforter around her, then stood on the stool and closed the window. A fine rain was falling outside. I turned on the electric radiator and moved toward the closet, trying to make sense of two accidents in two days.

"Zoe was very much alive last night," I said, apropos of nothing, pulling a pair of fleece pants off a hanger.

"Don't we all know."

"What do you mean?"

"She was a perfect bitch at *círculo*, pushing poor Danielle until she cried. I wanted to swat her cute little face."

"Who found her body?"

"Natasha went out for a run this morning. She saw her lying on a big rock at the edge of the water."

"Natasha went out to run in the *rain*?"

Zelda shrugged. "Russian brides have to keep fit. Anyway, she took the trail that goes along the bluff over the cliffs. When she came back, she saw Zoe . . . her body . . . in the water down below. Abigail called the sheriff. They're on their way over."

"She might just be unconscious."

Zelda shook her head. "Natasha said her face was in the water. And it looked like her arms and legs were cut. It's at least a hundred-foot drop. Please get dressed. Mimi's frantic. She thinks it's the locals trying to scare her into closing down the hotel. She wants to talk to you."

She stood up and moved toward the door. "Piero's making breakfast. Mimi wants to keep everyone in the hotel until the sheriff gets here. I'm going to go talk to Danielle, try to calm her down."

I hastily pulled on a blue sweatshirt and black leggings, padded down the hall to the communal bathroom. Frowning into the mirror, I washed my face and brushed my teeth and pondered the two accidents. Had someone deliberately dislodged the old railing and caused Eric's fall on the steps? And then had that same someone driven to Seattle to try to finish the job? Not likely. It was more conceivable that whoever tried to break into the I.C.U. at Harborview was deranged, and the assault on the nurse had nothing to do with Eric.

And Zoe's fall from the bluff: Was that the "something worse" referred to in the note on Mimi's desk? Had Zoe gone out for an early morning run and found someone lying in wait for her? Or had she simply stumbled and fallen from the bluff?

It's not uncommon for locals in remote communities to resent newcomers, but the hostility is usually manifested by malicious pranks. Air let out of tires, livestock that "wander" out of fenced pastures, sugar in a gas tank. Even the diverted barge of construction materials and the drifting boat fit that pattern. But murder?

I stepped into the silent corridor, hesitated, returned to my closet for my yellow foul-weather coat and boots. Mimi may have wanted everybody in the hotel, but if I was going to help her, I needed to see how Zoe had fallen to her death.

The light rain had turned heavy. I hurried across the courtyard, turned left, and followed the path around the hotel, found the trail I'd taken up to the meadow yesterday. The wind was out of the northwest, and as long as I was climbing, the steep hill provided some protection. Once I reached the top and started across the meadow, the gusts hit me with full force. Shivering, head down, I wished for another layer of clothing under the foul-weather coat. I hesitated when I reached the bluff where salal and Oregon grape obscured the steep drop to the huge boulders where white water was crashing. I squinted into the wind and rain, unable to make out anything below that resembled a body. I moved further along the trail and stopped beside a boulder that broke the force of the wind. Leaning against the cold granite, I scanned the shoreline. There was no beach, just boulders that had tumbled down the cliff over time. The tide was high. Heavy surf crashed onto the rocks. Again I scanned for a body and finally saw a small figure on the rocks that resembled a rag doll someone had hurled from the cliff. A few seconds later, a white cabin cruiser emerged from the mist and rain. The black lettering on the bow said SAN JUAN COUNTY SHERIFF'S DEPARTMENT.

The boat paused a hundred yards or so offshore. A red inflatable was lowered into the water, and two bulky figures in yellow foul-weather gear stepped down into it and rowed swiftly toward shore, where the small body was being pummeled with each incoming wave. Minutes later, Zoe's body was transported through the surf and gusting winds to the cruiser circling offshore.

I watched as Zoe's body was zipped into a body bag and lifted into the main cabin, wondering what time she had left the hotel. Most runners, particularly women, take care about when and where they run alone. Zoe was no dummy. Had she been so preoccupied that she'd run too close to the bluff, slipped, and gone over? Had she stepped too far out and had the bluff give way? Or had she encountered one of the hostile locals who decided to send

an even stronger message to the innkeeper of the
Dei Fiori?

I paced the bluff, scanning the trail. If there had
been footprints, the rain had erased them. In several
spots, the earth and stones had broken away, but if
the ground had given way beneath Zoe's feet, it
would be impossible to know exactly where. My
hands were icy and rain was running down my
face. I turned my back to the wind and trudged
back across the meadow, increasingly puzzled by
the death of the young TV woman.

A squarish, red-haired woman with a pleasant
face was standing by the fireplace in the great room.
Her yellow jacket said "S.J.C. Sheriff's Department." I nodded to her and went upstairs. Tacked
to the message board outside the dining room were
the two messages for Tiffany that I'd seen last night,
as well as one for Andrea and one for me from
Melissa that said, "Please call ASAP." I glanced at
the phone booth. Abigail was on the phone, waving
one arm as she talked, a deep frown between her
brows. The door to the hotel office was closed. I
heard a murmur of voices inside. I went into the
dining room. Serafina stood by one of the long windows overlooking the courtyard. Muttering to herself, twisting the white apron over her long black
cotton dress, she turned and went into the kitchen
where shrill voices were immediately raised in
Italian.

Still shaken from what I'd seen on the cliff, I filled
a cup with coffee from the big Thermos on the sideboard, added cream from the small white porcelain

pitcher, and was about to join the others at the table near the door when the dining room door opened. Mimi came in wearing a loose black sweatshirt over gray sweatpants. Her face was pale and tense. Through the open door I got a quick glimpse of Jeffrey Fountain, the San Juan County undersheriff, headed for the stairway.

I took a seat at the table with Andrea, Graham, and Tiffany. All three had somber faces, their eyes fixed on Natasha, who stood beside the table.

". . . not an accident," Natasha said shrilly. "This is murder. We have a murderer in the convent. We need the police." Despite the hysterical tone to her voice, Natasha, in fact, did not look particularly agitated, and it occurred to me that she was enjoying the melodrama, perhaps reenacting a scene from one of the books she translated. Romance on a remote island with a homicidal twist.

Mimi scanned the room and headed toward our table.

"Natasha," she said in a firm voice, "there is no murderer here. Please calm yourself." She turned to me. "Scotia, could we talk? In the office?"

I nodded and followed her out of the dining room with my coffee, past the phone booth, waited while she unlocked the office door. She transferred a stack of catalogs from the chair beside her desk to the floor and I sat down. She slumped into her chair with a long sigh and our eyes met. She shook her head. I reached out and touched her hand lightly. "How can I help?"

She closed her eyes momentarily and took a deep

breath. "I just met with Jeffrey Fountain, the under-sheriff. They've recovered Zoe's body."

"I know," I said. "I watched them from the cliff."

"You heard what I told Natasha, but I'm worried. She might be right. Zoe probably fell, but maybe she didn't. Maybe it's a horrible attempt to per-suade us to leave."

Her gaze wandered to the tallest stack of papers on the desk. She lifted the top sheet of paper and handed it to me. It was the hand-printed warning I'd seen the day before. "Piero found it shoved under the kitchen door yesterday."

"You should give this to the sheriff," I said. "If Zoe's accident was the work of a local, it could have been a malicious prank that went wrong."

"I already thought of that, but I also wonder if it's connected to Eric's accident. I talked to his sis-ter. She can't think of any reason why anybody would want to harm him."

We stared at each other in silence, then I asked, "What about Zoe's family? Have they been noti-fied? And where's Danielle? Has anybody talked to her?"

"Zelda is calling Zoe's family. Zelda and I tried to talk to Danielle right after Natasha discovered Zoe's body, but she went into a full-fledged panic attack and I gave her some of my medication. Stuff that was prescribed when my husband told me he wanted a divorce."

"When did Danielle last see her alive?"

She shook her head. "Last night apparently. But she was so incoherent, I can't be sure." She buried her face in her hands, then took a ragged breath. "The reason I wanted to talk to you is to ask if you would do some discreet investigating. See if you can find out if there's anything . . ." She fumbled for words.

". . . anything sinister going on?"

"I suppose you could call it that. And if it's local hostility, see if you can find out who and why."

"Have you ever had any *personal* contact with the local residents? Anybody ever threaten you in person?"

"Five or six people turned up for the hearing in Friday Harbor on the building permit. They had a petition with fifty names on it, which is just about every adult man and woman on Santa Maria. They claimed I was in violation of the Santa Maria Development Plan." She reached into the left-hand desk drawer, riffled through the vertical files, pulled out a bulky manila file folder. "This is the County Comprehensive Plan for Santa Maria Island. I've read it twice and I can't see that we're out of compliance with anything. We have our own dock. We pick people up at the ferry. Our guests don't bring cars to the island. We recycle. I've been buying supplies from the islanders whenever I can. Firewood, fruits, and vegetables. God knows, some of these people look like they could use the extra money."

I glanced at the thick tome and refrained from mentioning that attire in the islands was not always an indication of wealth. I'd seen more than one dotcom millionaire or aging philanthropist in dirty overalls. "So how did you get the permit?"

"The former owner had pushed through a permit for a bed-and-breakfast to accommodate up to twenty guests. It may have been before the County Plan was ratified. Anyway, we were grandfathered in. Nobody made any threats, but there weren't a lot of happy faces."

"Did you report the other incidents to the sheriff? The stonemason's boat? The missing supplies and tools?"

"Yes, but nobody came over. The woman who took my report said tools and supplies always disappear in the islands when construction is going on. Sort of a haves versus have-nots thing, I gathered."

"Zelda mentioned something about a delivery that went astray this week?"

"I was expecting a catalog order. Rugs for all the rooms, some new dishes for the dining room, new drapes for the library. Monogrammed robes for all the guest rooms. It should have been here two weeks ago. U.P.S. delivers once a week and leaves packages at the post office. The postmistress said she hadn't seen anything. Zelda checked with the shipper and they said the package was returned by the post office marked 'addressee unknown.' They're going to send it out again, but it's beginning to feel like war."

"What exactly do you want me to do, Mimi? Aside from the malicious mischief, if that's what it is, if you believe that Zoe's fall wasn't an accident, you should ask the sheriff to investigate it."

She bit the inside of her lower lip. "The under-sheriff said they're going to do an autopsy on Zoe.

But unless the medical examiner finds something suspicious, he doesn't think the sheriff will do an investigation."

"Did you tell him about the other pranks? Or ask him to talk to the guests?"

She shook her head, her eyes bleak. "I was afraid if he did the guests would leave and ask for their money back. And I've already committed it to the contractor who's finishing the upgrade on the rooms in the east wing. I can't stand any negative publicity at this point." She clenched her fists on the desktop. "I can't afford to fail, Scotia. I used all the money I got from the divorce settlement for the down payment, and I took out a construction loan for the renovation. If I lose this . . . I'd . . . have to go back to doing interior design in San Francisco." She lowered her voice to a throaty whisper. "I don't know what Piero would do, and I'd have to watch my ex-husband parading his slutty new wife to all our friends." She stood up. "I won't burden you with my personal problems. Could you kind of nose around the island and see what you can find out? Maybe if I knew who wanted me out, I could talk to him. Or them." She opened the desk drawer and pulled out a large checkbook. "I'll give you a retainer, if you like."

One of the hard-earned lessons that comes from being a private investigator is that there has be to a signed contract for investigative services, and a retainer up front. I looked at Mimi, thought about what her bank balance probably looked like, considered Eric, who was still in Intensive Care, and the blond-haired anchorwoman I'd seen zipped into the orange body bag. And despite the annoyance I'd been feeling over what I viewed as a lot of petty strictures and regulations, I broke own my rule.

"Let me see what I can find out informally. If I can have the registration forms and any personal information you have on the guests, I'll run background checks on everybody. And the staff as well. I'll need home addresses, Social Security numbers if you have them, and so on. We'll see what we come up with. When the rain stops, I'll take a walk around the island. See who wants you gone and why. And I'll need to go on-line with my laptop. So put your checkbook away for now."

Her face started to collapse. She squinted her eyes, but the tears came down anyhow. She wiped them away with one hand. "Thanks, Scotia. I'll tell Antonio you're going to use the van. It's a long way around the island." She lifted a key from the center front drawer of the desk, then went back to the file drawer and pulled out another folder. "This is the staff information. Zelda has the registration forms for the guests. She's working in the library downstairs. Use this office as long as you like. Just be sure to lock it when you leave. And would you ask Zelda to meet me in the dining room? We need to get the yoga sessions back on schedule."

I found Zelda behind the refectory table that served as a desk in the L-shaped library off the great room. The fragrance from the huge bouquet of purple lilacs in the cream-colored porcelain vase was heady.

It was part of Zelda's agreement with Mimi that

she would be on hand to deal with the day-to-day details of the seven-day retreat, and she'd converted a corner of the library into her own office space. I hesitated by the door, taking in the framed art print of Michelangelo's *The Creation of Adam* and the far wall that was dominated by a dramatic fresco depicting a meadow of red poppies. To my right was a floor-to-ceiling dark wood bookcase. Her long hennaed hair secured in a bun with two chopsticks, dressed in a flowered silk wrap blouse that looked as if it came from the pages of *Anthropologie* but was probably a thrift-shop find, Zelda had her back to the door. Her stockinged feet were propped on the credenza in front of the window while she talked on the phone and read from a Washington State ferry schedule.

"Saturday it leaves Friday Harbor at 2:45, gets here at 3:15." She giggled. "I can't wait."

Reluctant to intrude on what sounded like a private conversation, I moved over to the bookshelves and found a leather-bound collection of the works of Shakespeare and gilt-lettered editions of *The Canterbury Tales* and Bocaccio's *Decameron*. Another shelf was devoted to Italian novelists. I scanned the titles, reflecting with chagrin on how long it had been since I'd read anything even remotely resembling literature. Along with Di Lampedusa's *The Leopard* was Silone's *Bread and Wine*, Umbero Eco's *The Name of the Rose*, Moravia's *Two Women* and *Roman Tales*. I started to bend over to examine the italian cookbooks stacked on the bottom shelf when Zelda spun around, her hand covering the mouthpiece.

"Oh, hi, boss. Didn't hear you come in." Her face turned pink and she told whoever she was talking to she would call back.

"Sorry to interrupt, Zelda. Have you talked to Zoe's family?"

"No, I mean, yes. I mean I already talked to them . . . to her," she stammered. "To her step-mother. Zoe's father's in Europe at a conference. His wife, Zoe's stepmother, is going to track him down." She frowned. "The stepmother didn't seem surprised or upset when I told her. It was weird."

"Mimi's asked me to do some investigating about Zoe's accident. I'm going to order preliminary back-ground checks on the guests and staff. Mimi says you have the registration information."

She opened the right-hand door of the credenza. "I just happen to have that right here." She handed me two manila file folders and glanced toward the open door. "You want SSNs on Mimi and Piero?"

A year or so ago, suspecting that most of my clients lie to me in one fashion or another, I began including clients in the background check. "Can you get them?"

"I think so. I'll bring them to you."

"I'll be in Mimi's office."

"You need any help?"

"If DataTech turns up anything suspicious that requires your expertise, I'll let you know." Prior to setting up shop as a graphics artist and events ar-ranger in Friday Harbor, Zelda was employed by Microsoft—what she refers to as "my nerdy job"—and later worked for a computer security company in Seattle. Her technological expertise includes hacking e-mails and obtaining what is supposed to be unobtainable information from utility companies, banks, and various public agencies. Breaching fire walls is her specialty. I told her Mimi wanted to see her in the dining room and expected her to follow me out, but instead she turned back to the phone and speed-dialed a number.

Rita was cleaning my room when I got there. Her low-cut, cropped blue sweater left bare all of her belly down to her bikini line, as well as the top half of her small, creamy bosom. As she bent over the bed, her black pants clung to her tight little derriere. She watched me come in, ignored my greeting, and returned to making the bed as I retrieved my laptop from the closet. I wondered briefly what her problem was, then headed back to Mimi's office. The storm had blown over and bright sunshine illuminated the cluttered room. I started to read through the files on the staff and guests, and realized I hadn't had any breakfast that morning.

The dining room was empty except for Antonio, who was sweeping up, and Serafina, seated at a back table with a large white cup, bent over a magazine. I poured a glass of grapefruit juice and a cup of coffee, found a small box of Grape-Nuts and a banana, carried my tray to Serafina's table. She was reading *Time* magazine. In English.

"*Buon giorno*, Serafina. May I join you?"

She looked up, surprised, and nodded. "*Buon giorno, signora. Certo.*" She glanced at my bowl of cereal. "You miss *la prima collazione. Piero ha fatto un pan dolce.* Cinnamon buns."

I smiled and began to slice the banana. "I love cinnamon buns, but this is probably healthier for me."

She shrugged. *"La vita é breve."* She frowned. "The life was *molto breve* for Signorina Zoe. *Una tragedia, non é vero?"*

I nodded. "Zoe's death was a tragedy, yes."

She shivered. "This *isola* is dark. I feel death here. *La morte.* Bad people. When I walk on the path, no one smile. I go to the store and they look me like I am . . ." She shrugged.

I chewed my Grape-Nuts and once again flashed on the death of Adriana von Suder, the unlucky California wine heiress. Santa Maria Island had proved very dark for her also, and death had been waiting when she went off for her morning run. "Do you walk every morning, Serafina?"

"Si, signora. My *famiglia* is from the country. Every day we walk to the village."

"Did you go for a walk on Wednesday? The morning the photographer fell on the stairway?"

She nodded. *"Si, signora."*

"Did you see him go out alone?"

Her black eyes bored into mine, then she said, "I see nothing. *Niente."*

I thought about her comment to Piero yesterday. "Serafina, why do you think Eric's fall was not an accident?"

She frowned, looked away, and stood up. Pulling her scarf tightly around her shoulders, she stared out the window. The gardener was back in the courtyard. "I see it in the cards," she said. "A man, he is cruel to the animals. I tell Piero. He thinks I am . . ." She tapped her head. "You are *investigatore*, no? You will see. *La morte verrá ancora.*"

Death will come again. I silently repeated her dark prognostication and shivered.

She drew her scarf over her head and picked up the magazine. "*Arrividerci, signora.*"

"*Arrividerci*, Serafina." Wondering if she meant the unfortunate photographer was cruel to animals, I watched her disappear through the French doors, saw Natasha come in. The Russian translator, attired in a dark green T-shirt and matching leggings, poured a cup of coffee, added cream, and joined me at the table.

"The police? Do they talk to you?" she said. "Do they find the murderer?"

"We don't know that there was a murder," I said. "Did you have a pleasant evening with your friend?"

"John? Yes, very pleasant. He showed me his goat farm. After I do a massage for Andrea today, we are going to do a hike." She sipped her coffee and gazed absently out the window. "John wants me to leave."

"Leave the hotel?"

She nodded. "He thinks it is not safe here. He says I should move over to his farm."

"Because of the two accidents?"

"He says there are people here on the island who hate the innkeeper."

"Why do the island people hate Mimi?"

"She wants to change things."

"You mean like bringing in telephones? Or repairing the roads?"

She nodded and gave me a quick smile. "They are very silly. In Russia, no one says no to a telephone or better roads. Fifty miles outside of Moscow there are no phones."

"Does John also hate Mimi?"

"No, he also wants better telephones. He wants to sell goat milk and cheese on a web site. Now all he has is a cell phone that doesn't always work."

"Did John mention any names? Of the people who want Mimi to leave?"

She frowned and shook her head. "I do not remember."

"When you see John today, would you ask him?"

She finished her coffee and stood up. "I will ask him. And I also ask you a favor."

"A favor?"

"Yes. I am confused about this moving in together. Is that what American men want after one date?"

I laughed, thinking of more than one San Juan Island man who expected exactly that. At least according to Zelda. "I would have thought you'd be an expert on romance from translating the novels," I said teasingly.

She shook her head. "The people in romance novels are not real. Especially the men. They're . . ." She paused and I finished her sentence.

"They're fantasies. You're right. I'm not an expert on Santa Maria men, but you're a very attractive woman. As for moving in with you, John may have what we call 'designs' on you, or he may simply be concerned for your safety because of what's been going on between Mimi and the locals."

Natasha nodded. "I will have to find out. I learn quickly. I do not intend to go back to Russia."

There were now three messages for Tiffany tacked to the board along with the message for Andrea. There was no call back from Nick. On impulse I ducked into the phone booth, entered my credit card info, and dialed Nick's condo in Seattle.

"Hello?" It was a woman's voice. I'd heard it before. It belonged to Cathy, Nick's ex-wife. "Hello, who's calling?"

Slowly, without replying, I hung up the phone, assuring myself that with their daughter about to be married, Cathy had a legitimate reason to be in her ex-husband's condo and, at the same time, feeling more separate from Nick than ever before.

Thoughtfully, with an expanding cold spot in my solar plexus, I unlocked Mimi's office, stacked her papers on one side of the desk, and connected the laptop to the telephone line. There was one e-mail from Melissa. *What should I wear tonight? We're having dinner at some Spanish restaurant in the city. I'm so nervous.* I clicked on Reply and reminded her that something dark was always appropriate, maybe dark pants, a white silk shirt, and her black leather jacket.

A second e-mail was from H & W Security offering contact information for two private investigators in Trinidad. I chose the one whose address was the San Fernando yacht club and sent off an inquiry regarding her fee and availability in obtaining Harrison Petrovsky's signature on the estate documents when he made landfall in Trinidad. Then, putting my personal life on hold, I turned to the Dei Fiori personnel file and registration forms Zelda had given me.

Half an hour or so later, I'd composed a list of names and addresses of the retreat participants plus Joseph, and the same information plus SSNs for Antonio, Rita, and Gus. I had just clicked on the Data-Tech icon when Zelda came in and closed the door.

"I found an SSN for Mimi, but not Piero."

"How long's Piero been over here?"

"I'm not sure." She glanced toward the bank of filing cabinets by the door, two of which had keys dangling from the locks.

"I don't think we should start snooping in Mimi's files," I said firmly.

"Just give me a couple of hours," she said with a grin and disappeared through the door that led to the kitchen.

I transmitted the information I had on the participants and staff to DataTech, and was about to log off and disconnect the laptop when a new e-message arrived. I opened the message and smiled at the fluttering falcon. *Dinner at eight at the Empress Hotel in Victoria May 28? I can pick you up in Friday Harbor at the airport or wherever you prefer.*

The Empress Hotel is an impressive example of Edwardian architecture surrounded by green lawns, poised above the inner harbor of Victoria, British Columbia, which is just a few miles across Haro Straight from San Juan Island. Dining at the Empress is superb, and the upper-floor rooms have fireplaces and leaded casement windows that open onto the waterfront. Automatically, I started to decline, then thought about Cathy answering Nick's phone and about Nicole trying to reconcile her parents ever since their acrimonious divorce. Jaw clenched, I started to type an acceptance to Falcon's invitation, paused, shook my head, and felt tears behind my eyelids. I logged off my ISP, closed down the laptop, and headed wearily for my room. It was only 11:30 A.M., but I felt as if it had already been a very long day.

1

The window of blue sky over the island had widened and the wind whipped through the courtyard. I cut across the flagstones past the planters where the newly bedded geraniums cowered in the gusts. Rita had swept and made up my bed and closed the window. Fresh white towels hung on the rack next to the closet. I glanced at the window and recalled the conversation I'd heard last night between the two women in the room next door. Something about a gang? And something that was identical?

Hoping Danielle had recovered from her panic attack, I tapped lightly on her door, waited, knocked again. There was no answer and I returned to my room, wanting to attend Joseph's afternoon session, but also feeling pushed to find out more about Mimi's neighbors. I changed from leggings to blue jeans, pulled on my old white wool Arran sweater. Among the retreat registration materials I found a map of Santa Maria that indicated a store, a post office, and another small marina on the opposite side of the sound from the Dei Fiori dock. Beyond the store, the road bent to the northwest and dead-ended above the valley where Gus lived. There was no indication of distance on the map, but I thought I remembered the island was about five miles wide on each side of the sound, and probably ten miles long. I locked the strong wooden door, pocketed the big brass key, and headed out to make my acquaintance with the Santa Maria locals.

Downhill from the hotel, the road curved inland above the marina. I glanced down at *DragonSpray*; she seemed to be bobbing securely on her lines. Beyond the marina, the road began a slow rise to the southeast, curved again, and flattened out at Point Desperation, where I hoped to find the store. There was less wind on this side of the island and I regretted the choice of the thick sweater.

Half a mile above the store, I heard a motorcycle, and a minute or so later saw a large, dark-bearded man on an old Harley exit the parking lot in front of a shingled structure with peeling gray paint set several hundred feet back from the water. Atop the building, an American flag waved in the wind. The man passed without glancing in my direction and I had the strange feeling that I was invisible.

The tide was ebbing and a hundred feet of flat, gravel-strewn beach lay exposed under the midday sun. It was not a beach where children would ever build sand castles, nor would it ever make it onto the Travel Channel's list of America's most beautiful beaches. Which, I imagined, suited the residents of Santa Maria just fine. A dozen or so large logs lay washed up above the tide line. Above the high-water line, a dented aluminum skiff rested on its side, its concrete-block anchor buried in the mud and gravel. To the left of the store was a fenced pen filled with what looked like wild turkeys, the kind we used to have on San Juan Island at the county park before a major Hollywood production company made a movie there. Beyond the pen I glimpsed what looked like a solid wooden corral at least eight feet high with barbed wire strung along the top. It was the sort of enclosure islanders frequently used to protect a garden from marauding deer.

The sign above the door said SANTA MARIA GENERAL STORE AND U.S. POST OFFICE. To the right of the door was a smaller sign: BEER AND WINE. The hours of operation were eight A.M. to two P.M., Monday through Saturday.

Inside, a black wood-burning stove warmed the wood-timbered, high-ceilinged room. Beyond the eight or ten aisles of shelves sparsely stocked with groceries was a room filled with shelves of alcoholic beverages and a back exit, to the right of which were two closed doors, one with a white-lettered sign that said POST OFFICE. The sign on the other door simply said PRIVATE. A faint smell of frying onions mixed with cigarette smoke pervaded the store. From a World War II–vintage wooden radio above the counter drifted the unmistakable twang of Willie Nelson. The woman behind the wooden counter took a long drag on a cigarette, laid it in the brimming black glass ashtray on the end of the counter, and without speaking, regarded me with narrow blue eyes. No cheery "Good afternoon" or pleasant "May I help you" was forthcoming.

Her short hair, brassy blond with steel gray roots, was curly and unstyled, her tanned face lined with the wrinkles of a habitual smoker. A stained white apron covered a faded purple sweatshirt, which in turned covered her large midsection.

"Good afternoon," I said, taking in the two red Formica tables to the left of the counter, the makeshift sideboard with a commercial coffee machine and a brown electric crock pot with white soup dribbles on the side. Behind the woman I spied an old-fashioned soda fountain with pump-type dispensers like the ones I remembered from Fergie's Pharmacy at St. Anne's Bay on Cape Breton Island. A metal newspaper rack in front of the counter offered the *Seattle Times*, the *Friday Gazette*, and the *Santa Maria Sentinel*.

She nodded and took another drag on the cigarette. "He'p you with something?"

"Some lunch, perhaps?"

She nodded again, this time toward the blackboard propped on an easel beside the counter. Thursday's offerings were cream of mushroom soup and a ham-and-cheese sandwich on rye.

Basking in the warmth of Santa Maria hospitality, I ordered cream of mushroom and a Vernor's ginger ale, picked up a copy of last week's *Sentinel*, paid the woman five dollars and eighty-four cents, and obeyed her directive to help myself to the soup. Seated at one of the red Formica tables, I perused the *Sentinel* and sipped the soup, which was extraordinarily tasty. I told the woman so and received an unappreciative nod. Johnny Cash's "Folsom Prison Blues" drifted from two small overhead speakers.

The *Sentinel's* front page featured the Santa Maria Island School, a "remote and necessary school" that served eleven students from six families for the current school year. The students were in grades three to eight, and four would be graduating from the eighth grade in June. On the inside page, I studied the tide and current forecasts, found a recipe for Eloise's Carrot Cake and the weekly horoscope. There were three death notices and one birth notice. Johnny Cash gave way to a commercial for Gerber's baby food and the woman lit up another cigarette.

"What brings you to Santa Maria?" she inquired, fanning the cloud of smoke over her head.

"I'm staying at the hotel."

"Where you from? You don't look like a foreigner."

I hid a smile. It was true that when San Juan Islanders went over to the mainland, they referred to it as "going over to America."

"I live in Friday Harbor."

She tapped the ash off her cigarette and appeared about to pursue our scintillating conversation when the door to the right of the "Beer and Wine" annex opened. The man who stomped into the room was the one I'd seen on the Harley. Well over six feet, broad-shouldered, with red curly hair and beard, narrow blue eyes set too close together, brown canvas overalls over a red-checked wool shirt. Without glancing at me or the woman, he opened the Coca-Cola cooler and took out a bottle of Red Dog ale.

"You call the phone company?" He uncapped the bottle and took a swig.

"Couldn't," the woman answered. "No service this morning."

He scowled. "God dammit, Eloise, *call* the frigging phone company. Even if you have go over to Friday Harbor to do it. Remind them we do not want more phone lines over here."

"Right away, your highness." She took a drag on the cigarette and regarded him through half-closed eyes, a small smile on her face.

He scowled again. "The mail in?"

She nodded. "In and sorted. You got a letter from that law firm in Frisco."

"That'll be the hard-nosed lawyer the jackass from Sacramento hired."

"And the confirmation date on the pigs came."

The man uttered a colorful expletive and drained the bottle. He glanced at me for the first time, then at the woman, threw the empty bottle into the trash can, and disappeared through the doorway that said POST OFFICE.

"Your husband?" I asked.

She nodded.

"Appears he's having a bad day."

"He and Stuey got up early and went fishing. Stuey's our neighbor. Didn't catch hardly anything. Always makes 'em cranky." Eloise checked the contents of the crock pot on the sideboard and replaced the cover. "How many people staying at the hotel?" she asked.

I did a mental count, subtracted Eric and Zoe. "Six this week, I think."

She snorted with satisfaction. "Won't exactly make the mortgage payments with that, will she?"

I shrugged. "I have no idea."

"I heard there was an accident at the hotel."

I nodded.

"Some photographer from San Francisco, I hear. Fell down the stairs?"

I nodded again. So she hadn't heard about Zoe. I stood up. "You lived here long?" I asked.

"Five long years."

"You move over from the mainland?"

"Leroy was born here and he fished with his dad in Alaska till his dad died. That's where I met him. We lost the boat in a storm off Kodiak Island in '98. Then we spent some time in Colorado." She took a long drag on her cigarette and stubbed it out in the ashtray.

The Post Office door opened and Leroy reappeared, a bundle of mail in his big hand, a scowl on his face. "I talk to you in the office, Eloise?" He nodded toward the office door.

Eloise looked at my empty bowl. "I get you anything else?"

"No, thanks," I said, reaching for my rucksack. "I'm leaving."

She nodded and the two watched me hoist the rucksack over my left shoulder and depart. I closed the door, went down the wooden steps, and heard the dead bolt slide into place behind me. I checked my watch: 2:20. I'd overstayed my welcome in more ways than one.

I had planned to follow the road all the way around the island and loop back across the valley where Gus lived, but the rain started coming down again as I stood on the bottom step and contemplated the flock of turkeys lined up at the fence, hopeful of a mid-afternoon feeding. I pulled the hood of my parka over my head and trudged back to the hotel in the steadily increasing downpour, wondering how Eric was, wondering if the autopsy on Zoe had been done, wishing I was with Nick in Seattle, yearning to be anywhere but on Santa Maria Island.

It was nearly three thirty when I got back to the Dei Fiori. The rain had tapered off to a fine drizzle. Gus, accompanied by a large golden retriever, was planting what looked like lavender in the bed under a bank of windows outside the west wing. A figure in a long black hooded cape that could only be Serafina stood beside his kneeling shape. The two were in deep conversation; Serafina gesticulating wildly, Gus shaking his head from side to side. Apparently Serafina had made a friend. Or at least had found a companion in misery. Neither one noticed me and I slipped inside to the silent corridor.

It appeared the other guests were either dutifully attending the afternoon *mudra* session or were otherwise occupied. I left my rucksack in my room, hurried across the empty great room where the remains of an earlier fire were smoldering, and climbed to the second floor to check the message board. Zelda was about to lock up Mimi's office, a manila file folder under one arm.

"Hi, boss. I found what you wanted."

"Which was?"

"Info on Piero. Antonio took Mimi and Piero over

to Friday Harbor in the boat for diesel fuel and some supplies and a meeting with an electrician, I just happened to come across Piero's immigration file." She grinned and proffered the file folder. "I hope this helps, although I think the boy is clean. How was your tour of the island?"

"I met the people at the General Store. Their names are Leroy and Eloise. Eloise was anything but broken up about Eric's accident. Leroy's a native of the island, but I don't know their last name."

"Oh, yes. Eloise the postmistress. She's a real sweetie I hear." Zelda rolled her eyes.

"I don't have a good feeling about those two. Don't you have a friend in the post office in Friday Harbor?"

She nodded. "I'll call her and see what I can find out right after I talk to Danielle. She wants to leave the island."

"Does she know the next ferry's not until Saturday?"

"She does and she's not happy. By the by, Zoe's accident made it onto the noon edition of Fox News."

"Any word on Eric's condition?"

"Yeah, I almost forgot. His sister called and Angela called twice. Mimi wants you to talk to both of them. I'll leave the office open. Lock up when you leave."

I glanced at the file she'd handed me, with its dozen or so typed pages and handwritten registration forms. A pink message slip with my name on it was clipped to the manila folder. It was from Mimi. *Please call Eric's sister Patricia Szabo. Call Dep-*

uty Petersen. I moved a stack of magazines and a leather bound copy of *The Writings of St. Francis* and dialed the number for Patricia Szabo. She answered on the second ring with a breathless "Hello."

"Ms. Szabo, my name is Scotia MacKinnon. I'm a private investigator and I happened to be at the retreat on Santa Maria Island when your brother had his accident. Mimi Rossellini, the hotel owner, asked me to call you."

"I saw on the Seattle news that a woman was killed on Santa Maria. Zoe somebody. Was it an accident or is something weird going on up there? Did somebody try to kill my brother, too?"

"The sheriff hasn't yet determined the cause of death for Ms. Llewelyn. She did fall from the bluff. How is your brother doing?"

"He's out of the I.C.U. He's got a concussion, but there's no brain damage. I talked to him on the phone this morning."

"Has he remembered anything about his accident?"

"He just remembers slipping on the steps and grabbing at the railing. Then he says he must have blacked out."

"What kind of photography does your brother do?"

"Commercial things. He's gotten some big assignments for national magazines. I'm really proud of him."

"Do you remember any specific assignments he's had recently?"

"He did one for a champagne ad last month. They did it in the wine country, in Napa Valley.

And before that, he did a layout for a San Francisco architect for . . . I think it was *House and Garden*."

"Do you talk to your brother often?"

"Yes, I do. At least once a week."

"Has he mentioned any changes in his life? Anything that was bothering him?"

Silence. "It's sort of personal, but I think he met someone recently."

"Met someone, as a woman?"

"Yes. I think he was quite . . . smitten. He wanted me to meet her."

"Do you know her name?"

"No. I'm sorry."

"Any idea of her name or where she lived?"

"San Diego, I think. I don't know her name."

"Would it be possible for me to talk to your brother?"

"I'll give you the number in his room. Hold on."

She returned in a minute and I wrote it down.

"Ms. MacKinnon, do you think Eric's accident was . . . well, *not* an accident?"

"There doesn't seem to be any evidence that it was intentional."

I promised to let her know if any new information turned up, dialed the number for Eric's hospital room, listened to fourteen rings, then dialed the San Juan County sheriff's office.

Deputy Petersen was on another line. On hold, listening to dead air, I tapped my heel on the floor, impatient, wound up, anything but pleased at the way events were unfolding at the Dei Fiori.

"Scotia, what's going on at that retreat over there? One accident, one death, calls from the Seattle police, calls from reporters. Clue me in, for God's sake!" It was Angela, brisk and businesslike.

"What did the M.E. find on Zoe Lewellyn?"

"Two blows to the back of the head, major concussion, multiple contusions, fluid in the lungs. I saw the photographs. The blows to the head could have been made by a pointed instrument or by sharp rocks."

"Or by someone wielding a sharp rock."

"That, too. There were no fibers, no fingerprints on the body, no hairs except her own, nothing foreign under her fingernails. If someone pushed her, it would have been so fast she didn't have time to fight back. Who was she, anyway?"

"A TV talk-show host from Santa Barbara. What's the official cause of death?"

"Brain hemorrhage resulting from severe cranial blow."

"Estimated time of death?"

"Between two and six A.M. The woman's father has called three times, insists on an investigation. He mentioned something about his daughter being on suspension from . . . hold on . . . from KKSB in Santa Barbara, California. Said she was the victim of a smear campaign. Zelda says you've been retained sotto voce to do some investigating. You turn up anything yet?"

"I'm running background checks on the staff and guests," I said. "I'll interview as many as I can tonight. Is the sheriff going to investigate?"

"He says there's no reason to, nothing to indicate foul play. You know Nigel."

"Did you hear any more about the fracas at Harborview?"

"Nada. I think the conclusion was it was just some wacko, maybe didn't have anything to do with your photographer. But I heard they beefed up their security. Hold on." A click, then dead air. I tapped my heel on the floor for a minute or two before she was back. "Scotia, I've gotta go. We've got a domestic-violence incident on the ferry. Let me know what you turn up."

It was 4:20. I wanted to check e-mail, but my laptop was in my room. I locked Mimi's office and noticed that there were now four message slips with Tiffany's name. Someone she didn't want to talk to? A persistent suitor? I tried to remember when I'd last seen her. Yesterday at lunch? Last night at dinner? I couldn't recall seeing her this morning, but breakfast, such as it was, had been chaotic. I glanced around the upstairs hallway and checked for anyone coming up the stairway, then peered inside one of her messages. Then at two more. They were all from Roberto, the same man I'd spoken with briefly the previous day. The fourth message was from Tiffany's mother, also with no phone number. On an impulse, I removed the four pink slips, tucked the file on Piero under my arm, and headed for the west wing.

I tapped on Tiffany's door. There was no sound from within. I tapped again, waited, gave up, and unlocked my door. About to change into my flannel robe and head for the shower, I heard a knock on my door. It was Natasha, blue eyes shining, wide smile framing even white teeth. In one hand she held aloft a brown paper bag with the top of a bottle showing. In the other hand she clasped a terra-cotta bowl filled with ice cubes. "Vodka," she whispered conspiratorially, her face glowing. Her chestnut hair framed her face. "Do you want to accompany me for a cocktail?" She checked the corridor in both directions and nodded toward her room.

I smiled. In my early days in San Francisco, I'd developed a taste for vodka martinis, though now the only high-proof alcohol I drank was an occasional margarita. But given the events of the day— Zoe's body on the rocks, my chilly encounter with the proprietors of the Santa Maria Genral Store, no word from Nick—I made an exception. "Natasha, I would be delighted to accompany you. Give me five minutes to change for dinner and I'll be over."

It was closer to fifteen minutes because I couldn't resist riffling through Piero's file, which, at first glance, supported Zelda's contention that Mimi's handsome young husband was "clean." There was no Social Security number, but there was a number from Immigration and Naturalization that might help with a background check. Also several addresses and employers in Italy.

Two blue glass Mexican water tumblers sat on Natasha's bedside table when I joined her. I closed the door and watched her pour the colorless liquid over ice cubes. "You want it neat or with some vermouth?"

"With vermouth, please. Do you always travel with a full bar?"

"John got me the vodka and vermouth." She handed me a glass. "Mimi was in the kitchen," she said with a giggle. "I told her I needed the ice to make a compress for my headache." She raised the glass to mine. "*Za vashe zdorovye.*"

We clinked glasses and sipped the martini. "So, how was your hike with John?"

"We did not hike," she said. "One of John's goats, the nanny, had a baby last night. A kid, yes? John did not want to leave the little one, so we had our lunch in the barn. A stable picnic. It was romantic." She laughed. It was the first laugh I had heard all day, and it reinforced my intuition about her early-morning melodramatics.

"Where is John's farm?"

"In the valley, on Black Raven Road."

"Did you have an opportunity to ask John about the people on the island who don't like Mimi?"

"I ask, yes." She stopped, sneezed twice, and reached for the box of tissues on the bedside table. "The spa is too cold for me. It gives me sneezes." She sipped her vodka and frowned. "Here is John's list of the people who don't want Mimi here."

She stood up, pulled a sheet of paper from the pocket of the green canvas jacket in her closet. "These are the people that tried to stop the hotel."

The paper was a petition addressed to the Board of San Juan County Commissioners, requesting that the Commissioners deny the permit of Madeleine and Piero Rossellini to convert the existing structures on property in Subdivision 7, Plat 18, on the Island of Santa Maria to a bed-and-breakfast establishment. Among the hand-printed names beside the seven signatures were Leroy and Eloise Hausmann.

"Does John think any of these people had anything to do with Eric or Zoe's accident?"

She shrugged. "He says it is possible. Actually, what he said was, 'It is not *impossible*.' " She shook her head and smiled. "English grammar confuses me."

"English grammar confuses a lot of people, Natasha. Does John know the other people whose names are on the petition?"

"Yes, most of them. He said he could tell you about them." She sipped her drink in silence.

"You found her this morning, didn't you?" I asked.

"Yes. I run every morning. Yesterday she ran with me. I waited for her this morning for fifteen minutes, then I left."

"Was it raining when you left?"

"A little. I do not mind. It is so much better than Russia where sometimes I run in the snow."

"Did you see any other people around?"

She shook her head. "I went directly out the door here." She gestured toward the door at the end of the corridor. "I did not see anyone. I climbed up the hill and went through the Butterfly Meadow. I ran along the . . . what do you call it . . . the top of the land over the water?"

"The bluff."

"Yes, the bluff." She considered the word, frowned, then continued. "When I returned, I looked down and saw something white on a big rock and I saw it was a person. I came back and waked up Zelda.''

"Did you hear any noises in the corridor anytime during the night or early this morning?"

She considered my question, twisting a lock of chestnut hair. "When I went to the W.C. I heard a door close. I do not know which one."

"What time was that?"

"Maybe . . . 5:45."

Sunrise at this time of year was about 5:30. In the rain it would have been barely light. I shivered, thinking about Zoe running up the hill in the cold, wet grayness and angling across the meadow to the bluff, then either losing her footing on the eroding soil along the bluff or worse, suddenly being struck from behind, twice, then tumbling the hundred feet or so through salal and blackberry bushes to the huge boulders at the bottom of the cliff.

Nearby a door closed. "Excuse me a minute, Natasha. I need to talk to Tiffany." With the four pink messages I'd purloined from the board, I made a beeline for the door as Natasha reached for a *Vanity Fair* magazine and began flipping the pages.

I heard piano music from the other side of door number five. I knocked. "It's Scotia, Tiffany. May I talk to you?"

Five seconds passed, then ten. I was about to turn away in frustration when the door opened. Tiffany regarded me soberly, long blond hair swinging around her face. She tucked a strand behind her right ear and peered over my shoulder to Natasha's half-open door.

"What do you want to talk to me about?"

Her room must have faced onto the courtyard, but the drapes were closed. A purple windbreaker hung in her open closet. There was a pair of running shoes on the closet floor. A small, expensive-looking black duffel bag trimmed in red leather sat on her bed. On the luggage rack I saw a matching large suitcase, its cover open. It looked like Danielle wasn't the only guest eager to depart. "May I come in? I brought you these messages. I thought perhaps you hadn't seen them. One's from your mother."

"My mother?" She frowned, staring at the pink slips of paper in my outstretched hand.

"Perhaps you should call her."

"Yes, I will." She reached forward, closed her thumb and forefinger over the messages, and glanced at the cell phone lying on the desk. "Thank you."

"Did you enjoy the *mudra* session this afternoon?" I asked.

"I didn't go," she said softly. "I was afraid."

"Because of what happened to Zoe?"

She regarded me out of hazel-green eyes, then stared at the messages from Roberto and shook her head. Down the hall the door to number seven opened. Andrea came into the corridor and turned to lock her door. Tiffany peered into the hallway in both directions and motioned me inside. "I don't want to talk here," she said.

I stepped inside and she closed the door.

"What *are* you afraid of, Tiffany?" I asked.

She looked at the pink message slips she had

wadded into a ball. "I'm afraid of Roberto," she said softly.

"Who is Roberto?"

"My fiancé."

"Why are you afraid of him?"

"I want to break the engagement."

"What's stopping you?"

"He's not a nice man."

"I see."

She shook her head. "No, you don't," she said in a soft, vehement voice. She sighed and motioned to the bed. "Please sit down."

I glanced at my watch and sat on the end of the bed, wanting to turn the conversation to Eric and Zoe's accidents. "How did you get involved with this man?"

"I met him while I was on an assignment for *Travel and Leisure* at the Santa Anita racetrack. He had a horse running there. He came over and introduced himself, invited me to dinner. He's very handsome and very rich. He's also a total control freak and insanely jealous. I'm sorry. I don't know why I'm telling you this."

She took a deep breath, swallowed, and joined me on the bed. "I think I got involved with Roberto because of the way I grew up. I never knew my father. He was killed in Vietnam. We never had enough money, not for food, not for clothes. We never took a vacation. My mother had minimum-wage jobs. Fast-food places, cleaning houses. I *hated* it. She managed to save enough money to send me to college by working two jobs. When I started modeling, I sent her money and everything was fine until two years ago, when she fell down the stairs of her apartment building and broke her back. Now she's in a wheelchair."

"I'm very sorry."

"Roberto has been giving me money, a lot of money, so I can have full-time care for her."

"Was there no insurance money?"

"I hired a lawyer, but he couldn't prove any negligence on the part of the building owner. The stairs were well lighted. She had hospitalization insurance, and the owner's insurance paid her deductible, but we couldn't get anything for long-term care." She shrugged, chewed on her bottom lip. "So," she said ruefully, "I need Roberto."

"What's your degree in?"

"I don't have a degree. I was studying art history. Not very practical. When I was a junior at U.C.–San Diego, my roommate and I entered a beauty contest on a bet. I won, and got a modeling offer, then an offer from a small New York agency. I dropped out of college. I'm getting a lot of work now. Next week I'm going to Paris."

"And you still don't make enough to pay for your mother's care?"

She shook her head. "I can't seem to save anything. There's clothes and makeup and weeks at a spa to keep in shape. I'm probably a poor money manger."

I contemplated her dilemma. "Has Roberto ever harmed you?" I asked.

Without answering, she stood and began to pace the room. I watched her pad back and forth in her pale gray suede walking shoes with a tiny puma logo on the side. I sat in silence for a few moments, then stirred impatiently and thought about the file on Piero I wanted to go through before dinner, and the list of people who'd signed the petition against Mimi I'd been discussing with Natasha.

"Every woman thinks her life would be perfect if she were beautiful," Tiffany said slowly. "Well, beauty has a price. Roberto 'collected' me, like he collects antiques and trophy animals from his hunting in Africa. I'm for display, to impress his friends and business associates."

"Who is this Roberto? What does he do?"

"His name is Roberto Velásquez del Pino. What does he *do*?" She laughed mirthlessly. "He spends money. Oil money. Roberto is Venezuelan. He must have gotten on the wrong side of the president, because he had to leave the country. But he's got a lot of money stashed in this country. And I'm one of his passions, along with politics and his racehorses. I'm trapped," she said flatly. "And I'll be *damned* if I know what to do about it."

I frowned, thinking about the Venezuelan exiles Graham had mentioned.

"Mother lives in San Bernardino," she continued. "I'd have to move back there. I think I'd go crazy." She walked to the window and opened the drapes. "I tried to break the engagement a few months ago. Roberto flew into a tantrum. Said his women don't leave him. That if he couldn't have me, nobody would. It got . . . kind of ugly, but afterwards he apologized. He said he loved me so much, he couldn't stand the thought of losing me."

Considering how to redirect our conversation to Eric and Zoe, I remembered what Zelda had said about Tiffany having met Eric on a modeling assignment before the retreat. "Tiffany, I've been talking to the guests about Eric's accident. Did you know him before the retreat?"

"We met when I was doing a modeling assignment in California last month," she said, her eyes wary. "But I didn't know he was coming here."

"What was the nature of your relationship with Eric in California?"

She could have told me it was none of my business. Instead she leaned against the bureau and covered her eyes with her hands. When she took them away, her eyes were full of tears. "We . . . fell in love. He said I had to tell Roberto. He didn't understand that I couldn't. Not ever. That it was *impossible*. When I got back to San Diego and saw Roberto, I was afraid he would know something had happened. And I thought I would die when Eric turned up in Friday Harbor this week. I begged him to leave. I am so afraid Roberto will find out and do something to Eric."

"Does Roberto have any kind of a police record?"

She shrugged. "I don't think so. He's too clever. But one time he told me about waiting five years to get revenge on somebody in Caracas. I think he hired someone to kill the man."

I frowned. "Has Roberto ever threatened you?"

"A year ago I was scheduled to do an assignment in Italy. Robert thought the creative director had a crush on me and we had a big fight about it. He insisted on sending one of his bodyguards along.

The day before we left to come home, the director had a skiing accident. He died." She twisted her hands in her lap, shaking her head. "I keep expecting one of Roberto's goons to turn up here."

I considered mentioning the attempted break-in at the Harborview I.C.U., but decided not to. "If one of his goons turns up here, I think we'll spot him, Tiffany. First of all, there's no ferry until Saturday. The weather is too bad for a private boat to get in, and if anyone lands on the airstrip, the whole island would know."

She nodded. "You're right. I'm just being paranoid. Sometimes I think I'll go crazy. When Zoe got killed this morning, I thought maybe he did send someone and they got to her by mistake. Do you know how she died?"

"The cause of death was cranial hemorrhage, probably caused by hitting the rocks when she fell. The bluff is pretty unstable. And I think it would be hard to confuse you with Zoe." The warning dinner bell rang and I heard Natasha's door open and close. I stood up. "Do you remember when you last saw Zoe?"

She nodded. "I couldn't sleep last night. Andrea and I and Graham watched an old Bogart video in the library until about one o'clock. Zoe came in for a while. She seemed nervous and she left after half an hour. I never saw her after that."

The second dinner bell rang.

"Shall we go to dinner, Tiffany?"

She glanced in the mirror at her tear-stained face. "I need to fix my face. I'll see you there."

Tiffany didn't make it to dinner, nor did Andrea. Danielle sat by herself near the back of the dining room, picking listlessly at her pasta fusilli. From across the room, I watched her staring vacantly through the long windows at the dark storm clouds gathering against an orange-and-purple sky. It was the first time she'd surfaced since Zoe's death and I needed to corner her after the meal, find out if she knew where Zoe had gone and what she'd done after she left the library the night before.

I let the conversations flow around me; Graham and Joseph soberly discussing the Mideast situation, Zelda and Abigail making desultory small talk about quilting in the islands. Only Natasha's spirits were high, and I guessed that my abandoned martini had not gone to waste. Mimi was in and out of the kitchen; Serafina whispered to Gus at the table near the kitchen door across from a sulky Rita. When I left the dining room with Zelda a little after seven Danielle was lingering over her coffee.

"You find anything out about Eloise and Leroy?" I asked.

"The postmistress is Eloise Hausmann. She's married to Leroy Hausmann. He was born on Santa Maria, went to school in Friday Harbor, got in a lot of trouble in high school, and went off to Alaska to fish with his daddy. Leroy's not very popular on Santa Maria. A couple of years ago he turned in several of his neighbors for growing an illegal cash crop. You must have read about it."

I nodded, remembering the brouhaha about the sheriff bringing in the D.E.A. and that the people who'd been arrested for growing marijuana had gotten off due to a procedural problem with the evidence.

"Leroy was furious when the case was dropped, and swore the sheriff would regret it," Zelda added as Natasha followed us into the hallway. "Anyway, there's an issue about the whirlpool I have to deal with." She turned to the massage therapist. "Natasha, could we chat in the office?" She unlocked the office door and held it open.

"Zelda, I cannot bear a cold virlpool."

"In here, Natasha, please," Zelda said, even more firmly. Natasha shrugged, flounced through the open door, and sat in the chair beside Mimi's desk. Zelda started to close the door, then opened it again. "Scotia, I think Mimi would appreciate it if you could make *círculo* tonight," she said in a low voice. "She's pretty depressed and is afraid everyone is going to leave."

"I'll be there." I thought about the file on Piero I'd brought up in my bag. "Let me know when

you're done with the office. I'd like to check e-mail
and see if there's anything from DataTech."

"Thanks. Give me fifteen minutes." She rolled her
eyes, produced an impudent grin, and closed the
office door.

I loitered near the message board, waiting for
Danielle to emerge from the dining room. No messages on the board had my name on them, although
I imagined that Melissa had met her father in San
Francisco by now. I wondered what they had talked
about after eighteen years. The dining room door
opened and Danielle came out. I stepped forward.

"Danielle, Mimi asked me to interview the guests
about both Zoe's and Eric's accidents. Would you
have some time to talk this evening?"

She nodded. "I heard you were a private investigator. I'll get a sweater and meet you in the great
room in fifteen minutes."

"You've probably figured out that Zoe and I
were more than roommates," Danielle said without
preamble, curling up in the big leather chair in
front of the fireplace. I sat across from her on the
sofa.

"I seldom make assumptions, Danielle. Unless
I'm investigating a person, I believe people's lives
should be private." I took my tape recorder out of
my bag. "May I record our conversation?"

She frowned and stared at the recorder. "Does
that mean you're investigating *me*?"

"I'll be talking with all the guests and the staff.
I'm trying to find out how Zoe spent the time just
before her death."

"Are you doing this for the police or for damage control?"

"Probably the latter. Mimi is concerned for the safety of the guests."

"I prefer that you don't record it. What I have to say is not for publication."

I put the recorder back in the bag and pulled out a pen and notebook. She glanced at them and frowned, but didn't ask me not to take notes. "Did the police do an autopsy?" she asked.

"Yes. I haven't seen the actual report from the medical examiner, but the cause of death was a cerebral hemorrhage, probably caused by two blows to the head," I recited. "The blows could have been the result of hitting her head on rocks as she fell down the cliff."

"Or someone could have hit her on the head and pushed her over."

"Can you think of any reason for someone to do that?"

"If we were in Santa Barbara, I'd say yes. But not here."

"Who in Santa Barbara?"

She uncurled her long legs and stretched them toward the fire. "Zoe was an anchorwoman for the morning show on KKSB," she began. "She did it in a *Sixty Minutes* format, but with local stories. About three months ago, she had a guest on her program, a well-known Santa Barbara philanthropist who was . . . is . . . a homosexual. Zoe invited him on the show to talk about his collection of Polynesian art, then she began to question him about his . . . sexual preferences."

"Must have gotten great ratings for the show," I said dryly. "How did the gentleman react?"

"He was livid. He walked off the show and filed a lawsuit against the station the next day."

"Did he have a case?"

"His attorney thinks so. He says that what Zoe did amounted to slander and invasion of privacy. The station put her on suspension."

"For how long?"

"Until the case is settled."

"What is the name of the gentleman in question, the philanthropist?"

"Jeremiah Gonzales Bartholomew. A very rich man, well known and respected in the community. His grandfather was a rancher, one of the first settlers in the county."

I made a note of the name in my notebook. "Why did Zoe want to out him? Ratings?"

She shook her head. "It was more than that. Zoe was . . . I don't know . . . I guess you would call her *passionate* about honesty. She believed lying about your sexual preference or hiding it does a disservice to everybody else who is gay. She even wanted me . . ."

Her voice trailed off. I remembered the conversation I'd overhead last night. Danielle's distraught plea was beginning to make more sense. I finished the sentence for her.

". . . to come out of the closet?"

She nodded and the muscle in her jaw clenched tight. "I told her I couldn't do that to my family. Not to my parents or my daughters. It didn't serve any purpose except to further her own little crusade. *God dammit*, but she made me furious sometimes."

"What would have happened to you if you had done as Zoe wanted?"

"I would have lost my daughters. They've barely spoken to me since the divorce, anyway. It might actually have killed my father. His health is poor." She frowned. "And it didn't serve any *purpose* . . . except for Zoe's . . ."

Her voice faded. I studied her face, the high cheekbones, the wide brown eyes that were staring at nothing. Had she been furious enough with Zoe to push her off a cliff? Worried enough about her relationships with her family to silence the potential whistle-blower?

"When did you last see Zoe alive?" I said.

"She went out a little before midnight last night and I went to bed. I don't know when she came in. I got up once in the night, about two A.M. I didn't turn on the light, but I assume she was asleep then. When I woke up at 5:30, her bed was empty. I thought she'd gone for a run. Usually we ran together, but I twisted my ankle on Tuesday and on Wednesday she went with Tiffany and Andrea. I got sort of upset about that and we had a stupid argument."

"Do you have any idea where she might have gone last night before she went to bed?"

She shook her head. "I was too upset to ask when she went out."

"How long have you known Zoe?"

"A little over two years."

"How did you two meet?"

"I was president of the Historical Society. Zoe invited me to be a guest on her show to talk about the preservation program we were promoting. We wanted owners who remodeled or built new construction to consult us for guidelines. She was pretty hard on the owner of a new midtown construction project. After the show, she invited me to lunch. A long lunch. There was a . . . strong attraction between us."

She contemplated her fingernails, perfectly shaped ovals with pale pink polish. The nail of the index finger on her right hand was broken. She wore a thin gold watch with a mesh band. Her earrings were hammered silver and looked custom made. She swallowed. "I wasn't interested in boys in high school and, when I was in college, there was one . . . incident with my roommate. I ignored it, and then I met Marty, my husband. He's a good man, but my marriage had been dismal for ten years. Marty does international marketing. He travels a lot. When our youngest daughter left for college, he moved into one of the guest rooms and I kept busy with community work. When Zoe . . . came on to me . . . it felt good. Three months later, when Marty was in New Zealand, Zoe and I flew to Puerto Vallarta for a week."

Danielle stopped talking, stood, paced back and forth in front of the fireplace, hands in the pockets of her heavy beige cardigan. Somewhere a door slammed. I glanced toward the patio and saw Gus, his back to the entrance to the great room. He stood near the fountain and was talking to Tiffany. She listened for a few seconds and shook her head. Gus nodded vigorously, reached into his jacket pocket, and handed her a small package that she put in the pocket of her purple windbreaker. There was a sudden gust of wind, and rain began to pour down. Gus touched Tiffany on the shoulder and they separated, Tiffany running for the door at the end of our corridor, Gus trotting across the courtyard to disappear around the end of the east wing.

"After we came back, I told my husband I wanted a divorce."

I pulled my attention back to Danielle. "What was his reaction?" I asked.

"He said he had no objection to the divorce, but he wanted to stay in the house so our daughters would have a place to come back to for vacations."

"That was okay with you?"

"Not really," she said wistfully. "I loved the house. It was an old one we renovated, and the gardens were wonderful. But Zoe and I wanted to live together and I didn't want our daughters to know we were lovers. I thought it would be easier if he kept the house, so I moved in with Zoe. I told my family we were going to share her house until I found something else."

I considered what it would be like to live a double life, the stress and trauma of maintaining a facade. "Did your husband understand your relationship with Zoe?"

"He figured it out a few months ago. I think he was more angry than if I'd run off with another man. He couldn't believe I'd left him for a woman."

"What can you tell me about Zoe's family?"

"She was an only child. Her father was, or maybe

still is, an ambassador. Her mother died when she was a teenager. She doesn't get along with her stepmother. She hasn't seen them for as long as I've known her."

"Friends?"

"She was close friends with another couple in Ventura. I didn't care for them. All they could talk about was golf and their beach house in Ibiza."

"Did she have any enemies other than the unfortunate philanthropist?"

"Zoe's made a ton of enemies in her work."

"Can you give me any names?"

She hesitated. "When we first met, she was investigating a misappropriation of funds at the Santa Barbara symphony. She never found anything, but she ruffled a lot of feathers, particularly the chairman of the fund-raising committee. Last year, her crusade was some irregularity in records at the air pollution control office."

"Was she working on anything in particular when she got suspended?"

"She was. She said it was . . . I think her term was 'sensational enough' . . . to let her move to one of the big channels in L.A. or San Francisco. The other night she'd just found out something new about that story."

"You mean she'd found out something while she was here?"

"I think so."

"Can you remember any of the details?"

"It had something to do with gangs in Los Angeles. I'm sorry. I was angry about her working while we were on vacation. I didn't listen very carefully.

"Did anyone at the TV station know what she was working on?"

"You could try talking to her supervisor at KKSB. She might know. Her name's Janet Larson."

I made a note of the name.

"Scotia, I'd really like to get off the island and go home. It's terrible being here . . . in this room alone. I'm afraid to fly. My brother crashed in a small plane and I'm terrified of them. Could you . . . would you . . . possibly be able to take me to Friday Harbor on your boat? I would pay you."

I glanced out at the madrona trees tossing wildly in the wind and the rain beating against the windows. "Not a chance, Danielle. That's a nasty storm." I paused, shook my head. "Both my father and grandfather perished in an Atlantic storm. I have a very healthy respect for the ocean when it's acting up."

"I understand." She nodded, her eyes suddenly full of tears, and turned away silently. I watched her angular figure stride quickly across the great room. As she disappeared into the corridor, I speculated on her desire for an immediate departure and whether the relief of having to worry about being outed balanced the grief of losing a lover.

It was 8:45 when I got back upstairs. There were two messages on the board for me. One was from Mimi, asking if I had learned anything about the neighbors; the other asked me to call Melissa on her cell phone. Abigail was in the phone booth, her back to the hallway. I glanced at the office door. It was still closed and I didn't hear any voices on the other side. I knocked. There was no answer and it was locked. I pulled my cell phone out of my bag. The readout said "No Service." Surprise, surprise.

There wasn't time for a call anyway. If I was going to keep my promise to attend *círculo*, I'd have to wait until afterward to check e-mail and call Melissa, which I was looking forward to with mixed feelings.

9

All of us except Natasha, including Zelda and
Serafina, gathered in a semicircle in front of the
open fireplace in Il Refugio. I assumed Natasha was
nursing her cold or perhaps had gone off with her
goat herder. Someone had brought in sitting cushions and, instead of sharing our feelings, we listened to Joseph read more passages from Rumi. The
evening ended with Graham playing a short solo
piece called "Three Valleys" on his Japanese flute.
At any other time the music would have transported me to another dimension, but now it simply
provided a backdrop for my jumbled thoughts,
ping-ponging between uneasiness over Melissa's
dinner with Simon and trepidation that there was
going to be another "accident" at the Dei Fiori before I could find out who was behind them.

Leaving the others lingering near the flickering
fire, I slipped out of Il Refugio at 9:45. I hustled
along the path to the hotel, past the controversial
hot tub, dashed up the stairs to the phone booth,

and dialed Melissa's cell number. A recording advised me that the customer I was calling was out of range and invited me to leave a call-back number, which I did. As I exited the phone booth, Zelda unlocked the door to the office.

"Hi, boss," she said. "Sorry I left before you got back. Mimi wanted me to talk to Rita and Antonio. She thinks they're using *Gray Mist*, the hotel boat, for late-night rendezvous and getting drunk down there. Never a dull moment." She massaged her neck with both hands and sat down in front of the computer. "You find the message from your daughter? She sounded really pumped."

"I found it. Did you get the 'whirlpool issue' worked out?"

"God, just what I always wanted to do. Be a hot tub referee."

"What's the problem?"

"The usual temperature for a hot tub is around 104 degrees, and even that's too hot for some people. Natasha, however, claims it's not therapeutic unless it's at least 108. Tiffany swears she'll look like a boiled lobster if she gets into water that hot. Abigail says the two almost had a fistfight last night." She typed two lines and clicked on the printer icon.

"Did you reach a compromise?"

"I told Natasha it's to stay at 104 degrees. Period. She went out muttering about Nazis." Zelda extracted a printed page from the printer tray. "I'm done with the computer if you want to get on the Internet. I'm going downstairs to do horoscopes and make copies of tomorrow's agenda. Then I'm off to bed." She was almost out the door, then chuckled and turned back. "Abby talked to one of her friends in Friday Harbor today. Remember the judge's wife who wanted you to investigate her hubby because she thought he was involved in hanky panky with his law clerk?"

"The wife who'd been sleeping with the gillnetter?"

"Yup. Well, guess what? The gillnetter's wife and the judge just announced they're getting married. See ya."

Smiling over the vagaries of romance in a small town, thinking that ten o'clock was early bedtime for Zelda, I logged on to my Internet service provider over in Friday Harbor and clicked on the "web mail" button. There was only one new message. It was from DataTech with brief background reports on the guests and staff.

A quick scan of the five reports confirmed the bits and pieces of data I already had on the retreat participants. None had police reports. Gus had lived on the Kitsap Peninsula until ten years ago when he'd moved to Santa Maria. The only thing out of the ordinary was that his stepdaughter had disappeared at age fourteen, three years before he was divorced from the girl's mother. The report on Rita included an arrest for shoplifting at a Spokane supermarket when she was 12, but charges were dropped. There was nothing on Andrea Cross nor on Antonio Tozetti, the van driver. However, there was a report on an Anthony Bustamante of Los Angeles who had the same SSN as I'd been given on Antonio. Anthony Bustamante had several moving violations in Los Angeles, but had never been arrested.

I printed out the reports, then supplied DataTech with the INS information on Piero as well as his addresses and employers in Italy, and ordered in-depth reports on Piero as well as on Eric and Zoe. I was puzzling over the lack of information on Andrea when the phone rang. It was Melissa. Zelda was right about her being pumped: she sounded like she was running on pure adrenaline.

"Mom! What took you so long to call back? I called over an *hour* ago."

"Sorry, Melissa, I couldn't get a phone." I took a deep breath. "So, how did the dinner with your father go?"

"It was *so* cool. He took me to this great Spanish restaurant called El Greco. We had tapas and paella. And for dessert there was crème brulée and then we went to the Skylounge at the Top of the Mark. And he *danced* with me," she ended with a slight squeak to her voice.

The Mark Hopkins is one of San Francisco's legendary landmarks. The lounge on the nineteenth floor has an incomparable 360-degree panoramic view of the city, San Francisco Bay, and the Golden Gate Bridge. Nick had taken me there on our second date.

"Mother? Are you there?"

"I'm here, Melissa. I'm glad the evening went well."

"He looks almost like I remembered from your old pictures, but he's even more handsome." She paused for a minute, then said, "The reason I called you from the city was that Simon wanted to talk to you."

So it was Simon, not "Dad" or "my father." "Why did he want to talk to me?"

"Mother! He was your husband! He said he missed you."

"For *eighteen years* he missed me?" I said angrily. "So why didn't he come back? Come on, Melissa. He's the one who went away and left us."

"He said he thought you weren't interested in him anymore. That you were too busy to be with him."

Too busy to be with him! "What did he expect?" I snapped. "I had you to take care of, I was a full-time student, and I was working twenty hours a week to keep food on the table while he did his student politics! And your father was not exactly into cooperative child care."

There was a silence, then she said, "He says he asked you to go with him to the Seychelles."

I thought back to that awful summer eighteen years ago. Melissa had been sick a good part of the spring with a low-grade virus. I was a junior at San Francisco State and I'd missed a lot of classes to take care of Melissa. Simon was a year ahead of me and deeply involved in campus politics. He had graduated with a degree in Criminal Justice, and the graduation gift from his parents was a three-week dive trip to the Seychelles. A dive trip for one. It was true that we had briefly talked about my going along, but we didn't have the money for my fare.

"I couldn't go with him because there was no one to leave you with," I said wearily. "And we didn't have money for my ticket." Simon had wanted me to use the money I'd saved for my next year's tuition, but I had resisted. More importantly, his parents were leaving on a cruise to Norway, and my mother and Giovanni were in Italy, so there was no one to leave Melissa with, even if she had been healthy enough to leave, which I thought she wasn't.

"He says you could have borrowed it."

"Melissa, it wasn't that simple."

"What do you *mean*, it wasn't that simple? He was your *husband*. You should have gone with him. You could have taken me. If you had, we'd . . . we'd . . ." Her voice broke and she started to cry. "We'd still all be *together*. We'd have been a family all these years. The divorce was all your fault. I don't even want to *talk* to you."

She broke the connection. I stared at the phone in my hand, speechless, desolate beyond description. Slowly I replaced the handset in the cradle and backed out of the phone booth, my heart pounding. Was she right? Should I have used my tuition money for that long-ago trip? Was it my duty to pack up a sickly five-year-old and traipse halfway around the world to accompany my husband on a dive expedition? If I had, would he have insisted that we stay there? Would I have ever finished my degree? What would have happened to me and Melissa?

I gathered up the DataTech reports, logged off the Internet and locked up Mimi's office. From below, I heard Abigail's voice in the great room, then Zelda's laughter. I leaned against the wall next to the message board for several minutes, my hands over my eyes, tears trickling between my fingers. Downstairs a door opened and closed, then silence. I took a deep breath, wiped away the tears, and headed for the stairway, praying I wouldn't run into anyone.

PART 2

For the female of the species is more deadly than the male.

—Rudyard Kipling

10

"What do you mean, Tiffany's *gone*, Rita? Where has she *gone*?"

It was Friday morning. Mimi's clipped syllables cut through the small conversations in the dining room, where *silenzio* had been abandoned. She stood beside the half-opened door to the kitchen, dressed in the same black trousers and black shirt she'd worn the night before. Her pale, tense face was devoid of makeup, her long hair caught up in a tortoiseshell clip on top of her head. Mimi's crisp words were addressed to our chambermaid, who was leaning nonchalantly against the French door leading to the hall, vigorously chewing gum, her arms folded over her white T-shirt whose inscription read, *There's no such thing as a good morning. They all begin with waking up.*

"How the hell should I know where she's *gone*?" The heads of the retreat participants, most of whom were about to finish their breakfast, swiveled toward Rita. The thin, young woman with curly black hair in skintight blue jeans shrugged. "She's not in her room. That's all I know. The door was locked, window's open, and the effing floor was all wet. Maybe she had a hot date."

Mimi narrowed her eyes and glanced at the rain coming down in sheets in the courtyard. Somewhere outside a door banged in the wind. "Are her clothes still there?"

"They're all packed up in her fancy suitcases."

"Was her bed slept in?" This question came from Andrea, who was sitting beside me. I glanced around the room, noting that, in addition to Tiffany, Zelda and Natasha were also absent.

"It's not made up, if that's what you're asking."

"Are you quite sure you checked the right room, Rita?" Joseph asked gently.

Rita snapped her gum and nodded. "I'm positive. Room number five. I work here, remember."

"There's no need for rudeness," Joseph said, folding his napkin and pushing his chair back. Rita's face became a shade more petulant as she slowly blew a pink bubble. Before it could burst, she shrugged and disappeared through the French doors. Listening to her steps go down the stairway, I wondered how she dared be so insolent to her employer.

"I'll see you all in Il Refugio at 9:30," Joseph said. "Let us hope that Tiffany has simply gone for an early morning walk." He stood and headed for the door as Zelda came in. Mimi said something to Antonio, who immediately left the room through the kitchen door, then she motioned to me, met Zelda at the door to the hallway, drew the two of us into the office, and closed the door.

"What did I miss?" Zelda asked, her eyes moving from Mimi's face to mine. Her hair was wrapped in a neat twist high on her head, her skin was dewy, her green eyes sparkled. Early bedtimes seemed to agree with her.

"Tiffany's missing," Mimi explained wearily. "I didn't see her all day yesterday. I asked Rita to check her room and make sure she was all right."

"I talked with her last night just before dinner," I said.

"Was she okay?"

"Not exactly okay. Seems she has a jealous fiancé that she's afraid of."

"His name's Roberto," Mimi said. "He started calling at seven this morning. He's threatening to call the police if he doesn't hear from her by noon."

"So his fiancée is on a retreat and doesn't want to use the telephone," Zelda said. "What's the big deal? Is this dude a weirdo or what?"

"Not so weird if you know Latin men," I said. "I get the impression he keeps a twenty-four-hour watch on her."

Zelda nodded. "Actually, she told me Roberto once sent a bodyguard along when she was on a photo shoot in Italy. I thought she was joking."

"Possessiveness is no joke," I said. "Her fears are real, but where did she go? And in the pouring rain?" I flashed on the encounter I'd seen while talking with Danielle last night, wondering what Gus had given Tiffany in the small package. "I saw her talking with Gus in the courtyard about seven last night, just before the rain started. He gave her a package. Is he here today?"

They both shook their heads. "He called and said the road is flooded," Zelda offered, and then smiled. "I think Gus has a crush on Tiffany. He calls her 'the lavender butterfly.'"

"She can't have gotten off the island in this storm," Mimi said. "There's no way."

"What about Natasha?" I asked. "She wasn't at breakfast either."

"Natasha has a cold," Zelda said, "which is apparently all my fault since the hot tub is *only* 104 degrees. However, I notice the cold didn't stop her from heading out for a rendezvous with her goat herder last night."

Mimi sighed. "Maybe Tiffany is with Natasha."

"I don't think so," I said grimly. "I'll take a close look at Tiffany's room. Can one of you check the other rooms? And then we should search the rest of the island as soon as possible."

Mimi handed me a key. "This is the master key. After you check the hotel, you two take the van. I'd go with you, but I want to speak with Rita about her attitude, and I'll need to let the guests know we need to search the rooms." She glanced at Zelda. "You remember I thought Rita had something going with Antonio?"

Zelda shrugged. "Mimi, I'm not sure anything's going on. I chatted with them both last night, separately. Told them to cool it, at least until the retreat is over. It's probably why Rita was so bad-tempered this morning. Actually, Antonio said he'd never laid a hand on the woman; that he's got a girlfriend in L.A. I think his words were, 'I wouldn't be caught dead with such a skinny bitch.' "

Mimi said, "So how do you explain the cabin lights that were left on on *Gray Mist*? Or the empty beer bottles rolling around the cabin and the dead battery? Graham and I tried to move the boat to the other dock out of the wind before breakfast and we couldn't start it. Scotia, Graham said you're good with boats. Would you take a look at the battery and tell me if there's anything we can do? I don't think Gus is going to make it to work today." She glanced out the window at the red branches of the madronas whipping furiously in the wind. "Not that I blame him. It's not exactly gardening weather."

"How do you usually keep the battery charged?" I asked, realizing that, since the island was off the grid, there wouldn't be a shore power line that the boat could be plugged into to keep the battery charged.

Mimi shook her head. "Look, I don't know anything about boats. It came with the property and Gus always took care of it. I think he just charged the battery by running the engine. It was never a problem until now."

"Can you send someone to check the meadow and the bluff trail where Zoe fell or was pushed?" I asked.

"That's where Antonio went."

I glanced toward Mimi's computer. "I'm expecting background reports on Zoe and Eric," I said.

"I'll check them for you, boss," Zelda said, "while you check out Tiffany's room."

It was a little after ten o'clock when I returned to the west wing. Master key in hand, I knocked on Tiffany's thick door. "Tiffany, it's Scotia. Are you there?" I half expected to hear a tentative voice within, but there was only silence. I knocked again, waited, and then unlocked the door. The room felt cold and damp, but the bed was made up and the floor dry. Despite her insolence, apparently Rita had returned to the room. Unlike my room, with its high clerestory windows, Tiffany's windows were long and opened directly onto the courtyard. She must have left in a hurry to have left one open in the rain. Or been carried out by someone who didn't bother to close the window.

I pushed aside the drapes and examined the edges of the window frame for fabric threads but found none. A large packed suitcase lay zipped closed on a luggage rack. Below it was a black duffel bag. The purple windbreaker I'd seen in the closet the night before was still on its hanger. I didn't see the gray suede walking shoes she'd been wearing when I talked to her.

I unzipped the suitcase, searched through the layers of clothing, and found lacy lavender lingerie, a pair of designer blue jeans, a purple leotard, a man's white dress shirt. Under the neatly folded silk trousers in various shades of lavender and mauve were matching silk shirts. In a side pocket I found a book of matches from a restaurant in St. Helena, California, with a San Francisco phone number written inside. I guessed the number was Eric's. Tucked inside a gray leather purse was an empty envelope addressed to Tiffany at the St. Helena Inn. The postmark on the envelope was La Jolla, California; the return address was "R. Velásquez del Pino, 23 Camino de los Arboles in La Jolla." Speculating on what the letter had contained, I copied the phone number and the address into my notebook. About to zip up the luggage, I spied what looked like a sheet of white paper on the very bottom. I moved the clothes aside and starred at a stunning, elegant black-and-white nude photo of Tiffany. She was sitting on an old wooden chair, gazing out a window at a vineyard beyond, her slender body stretched toward the camera, her hair a luminous white mane in the sunshine. I imagined it had been taken while she was on the recent modeling assignment. I turned the photo over. It was no surprise to see the "Eric Szabo Photography" imprint on the back. I replaced the photo and zipped up the suitcase, shuddering to think of what Roberto might do if he found the photo.

The small duffel bag contained a pair of sandals, a Nikkon digital camera, a small black leather case of jewelry, a black-and-white photograph of a man who looked like a Latin Clark Gable, and a smaller cosmetic case of lavender quilted cotton filled with high-end beauty products, the kind that cost several hundred dollars just to "sample" the line. I checked the smaller bag again, looking for pajamas or a nightgown, and found neither. She either slept in the buff or had departed in a nightgown or pj's.

I played with a number of worst-case scenarios

to explain her disappearance in the context of the week's events. Worst case scenario Number One was that someone—Leroy, or his buddy Stuey—had pushed Eric down the stairway and Zoe off the cliff in order to scare Mimi into leaving the island. Scenario Number Two—less likely—was that Eric's fall was an accident and the involuntarily outed philanthropist from Santa Barbara had Zoe followed and pushed off the cliff. Scenario Number Three had a number of permutations and combinations of Number One and Number Two, including Tiffany in her paranoia fleeing the hotel, either voluntarily or otherwise, and suffering some yet-undiscovered "accident" at the hands of Leroy Hausmann. Other scenarios considered Tiffany being kidnaped for ransom, which was hard to fathom, given that virtually no one on Santa Maria except for Zelda, Mimi, and I knew there was a woman at the Dei Fiori whose fiancé was wealthy.

The wind was still gusting, but the rain had ceased, at least momentarily. It was a good time to check out Mimi's boat. I locked up Tiffany's room, collected a sweater and yellow foul-weather jacket from my room, and headed out to troubleshoot the battery problem on *Gray Mist* before the next monsoon arrived.

The hotel grounds were deserted. On my way out I checked under Tiffany's window for possible footprints. If there had ever been any, the heavy rains had washed the flagstones clean. There was not the tiniest clue to indicate where the blond-haired supermodel had gone, or with whom.

*   *   *

Down at the tiny marina, *Gray Mist*, a battered aluminum power boat twenty-five or thirty feet long with an interior cabin, powered by a forty-horsepower Mercury outboard, was bouncing on her lines. The vessel was properly tied, with bow and stern lines and two spring lines. Three dirty white fenders tied to the side of the boat were doing a good job of protecting her from damage, but she was being driven hard against the wooden dock by each gust of wind and clearly needed to be moved if the wind continued to build. From the dock I could see that two or three inches of water had collected in her cockpit, so I climbed aboard *Dragon-Spray* and changed into my boots before attempting to board *Gray Mist*.

There was no response when I turned the ignition key. I unlocked the sliding door and stepped into the small cabin. The interior was anything but inviting, and I couldn't imagine a less likely spot for a romantic tryst. I picked up the incriminating beer bottles and put them in the galley sink, then began searching under the tattered and dirty seat cushions for a battery locker in hopes of finding that the electrical system had been wired with a backup battery.

Apparently Graham was as uneducated about boats as Mimi, since neither of them had found the Perko switch mounted on a bulkhead beside the circuit breaker box. I moved the switch from battery one to battery two, made sure all the other circuits were shut down, then climbed up to the cockpit and turned the ignition again. This time the motor caught and, after a series of coughs and sputters, the big engine leaped to life. I glanced around the dock, wishing I had some help with the dock lines, and spied John Jordan nosing his small power boat into the dock. Natasha was with him, bundled in a navy blue quilted parka, a black watch cap pulled over her auburn hair. She smiled and waved. I returned her greeting, stepped off the aluminum boat, and caught the line John threw to me. I wrapped it around a cleat to stop the motion of the boat, and held it while John jumped off.

"If you're thinking of taking the boat out, I'd recommend against it," he said, taking the line from me and cleating it off. "It's not so bad on the other side of the island, but on this side the tide is running against the wind, and it's nasty."

"I want to move it closer into the cove, maybe get out of some of the wind, if you could give me a hand with the lines."

He nodded and began to untie *Gray Mist*'s spring lines. Ten minutes later we had her moved to a more sheltered spot and retied. I put the transmission into neutral, pressed the button that would tilt the big Mercury engine out of the water, turned off the power switch.

"Can I sneak back into the hotel without getting whipped?" Natasha asked with a smile.

"I think Mimi is well occupied this morning," I said, "so you're probably safe. But Tiffany is missing. Have you seen her?"

John gave me a sharp look and frowned. Natasha shook her head. "I haven't seen her since yesterday. Where could she have gone?" She shivered. "Scotia, do you think—?"

"Tasha, let's go get your stuff," John interrupted.

"I have to get back to the farm. We're sure to have two more new kids today." He headed for the ramp.

Natasha looked apologetic. "Scotia, I'm moving out of the hotel. To John's place."

I nodded, not surprised. "Probably a good move." Although Mimi wouldn't be happy about losing her massage therapist.

At the foot of the ramp John paused and looked back at me. "If you want to come over to the farm later, we can talk. It's two miles beyond the store on Black Raven Road. Look for a red barn."

I nodded and watched Natasha climb the ramp behind her bearded friend. It was 11:20. I went into *Gray Mist*'s cabin to turn the electrical switch back to number one battery, in case there was a bad circuit on the boat that might deplete the good battery. I gave a last look around the cabin and was about to leave when I saw what looked like a piece of red silk fabric on the dirty cabin floor.

It looked incongruous in the surroundings and I surmised it must have fallen from under the cushions when I'd been looking for the batteries. I looked closer and picked it up. It was a pair of men's underwear, bikinis actually, probably size 32 or 34, and I wanted to giggle. So that was what Antonio wore under his urban-cool black outerwear. Red bikinis. So much for his protestations of innocence.

I tucked the forgotten undergarment into a white plastic grocery bag that had probably been used for transporting the beer, gave a final check around the cabin, and locked up.

*   *   *

One of the pink slips with my name on the message board was from Nick. The other was from Melissa. I slipped into the empty phone booth and dialed Nick's cell phone number. He answered on the first ring. He was on his way to the formalwear store to pick up his tuxedo. The prenuptial agreement had been signed, but Nicole and Larry, her fiancé, had created a stir by disagreeing on last-minute changes in the vows.

"I know you wanted to come down, Scotty, but it's been a bear. Last night Nicole got cold feet and wanted to call the whole thing off. Cathy had a panic attack. Larry's parents are divorced and refuse to be seated in the same church pew. Believe me, you're not missing a thing. The reason I called is that I talked with my assistant this morning and she said KIRO-TV had an item about two accidents on Santa Maria Island this week. A photographer who fell down some stairs and a woman who fell off a cliff? Is that near where you are?"

"Unfortunately, yes." I filled him in on the details of Eric's and Zoe's 'accidents.' "And this morning another guest is missing. We're hoping she'll turn up."

"Good grief. How much longer is this retreat supposed to last?"

"Until Tuesday. I've agreed to do some investigating for the innkeeper."

"Any reason to think there's foul play involved?"

"It's hard to say. The stairway Eric fell down was a disaster waiting to happen. The cliff Zoe fell from is treacherous along the edge. But Mimi's had problems with the locals ever since she started renovating the hotel."

"I've heard some of the back-to-the-landers in your neck of the woods can be pretty intransigent with newcomers. She has my sympathy." He paused and I heard traffic noises in the background. "The main reason I called, Scotty, is that I thought I'd take a few days off after the wedding. Nicole and Larry are staying at my condo until they leave for a honeymoon. I don't have to be back at the office until next Friday. Any chance you could get away on Sunday? We could go to Victoria or stay at that great hotel at Oak Bay. Maybe even get a glimpse of Nessie's cousin, the cadborosaurus? What do you think?"

I laughed. Sightings of a green, fast-swimming, part-reptilian, part-mammalian sea creature had been reported in the waters surrounding Vancouver Island for a century. And the old country inn was one of my favorites. I hesitated, still rankled by the vacation-girl syndrome that kept me in the background whenever Nick's family was involved, but still unable to turn down the opportunity to spend time with the handsome attorney who had been the love of my life for so many years.

"Scotty? Are you okay? Could you finish up your investigation and get away?"

"Nick, either I find out in the next twenty-four hours what's behind all the accidents, or I'm going to suggest that the retreat be canceled. So, yes, going to Victoria and looking for cadborosaurus sounds great!"

"There should be some breathing room this afternoon before the rehearsal dinner tonight. I'll make some phone calls, see if we can get in at the Oak Bay, maybe arrange a side trip over to the west coast. We've been talking about going to Tofino for years." He promised to call back by evening, and I returned Melissa's call.

"Mummy, I've been thinking about the mean things I said last night. I was just feeling very . . . sad. About not having a father when I was growing up. I talked to Simon this morning, and I don't think he ever meant to come back to San Francisco when he left us. It wasn't very responsible of him." She paused. "So please don't be mad at me."

"I'm not mad at you, Melissa. I'm sorry that it turned out the way it did."

"Grandma's called twice; she wants to talk to you. She saw something on the news about a woman getting murdered on Santa Maria. Did that really happen?"

I told her I was checking into it for the innkeeper and she said she was off to class. My mother lives down in Mendocino, on the California coast, with her long-term partner. I got her recorder and left a message that I was safe and well. As I left the phone booth, Zelda came pounding up the stairs, red hair flying around her still-radiant face. I pulled the white plastic bag with the red bikini underwear from my jacket pocket and handed it to her.

"What's this?" she asked.

"A little item I found on *Gray Mist*. You or Mimi might want to return it to Antonio."

She pulled the underwear from the bag and burst

out laughing. "The young man is an accomplished liar. I'll give them to Mimi and let her do the honors." She unlocked the office door. "Incidentally, Mimi fired Rita this morning. Said she doesn't like her attitude. Rita's leaving on the ferry tomorrow. I have to get a want ad on-line right away or I'm going to be mopping floors and making beds. Maybe we can get a replacement before the summer season starts in Friday Harbor. Oh, yeah, these are the two in-depth reports from DataTech on Zoe and Eric. I haven't had a chance to look at them."

Reports in hand, I moved into the dining room, where lunch was laid out on the sideboard. I was the first one in, so I assumed that the morning yoga session was running late. I helped myself to what looked like tuna fish salad with celery and raisins, and a slice of warm banana bread, filled a white coffee mug, and sat at the table next to the window in the corner.

Beneath a sky heavy and overcast, a strong southeast wind whipped the new plantings in the courtyard, but for the moment no rain fell. As I watched the courtyard, Mimi and Graham, both wearing dark blue rain ponchos, came out of the main door, followed by Mao. Heads down, they hurried across the courtyard and disappeared around the east end of the building. Mao leaped off the veranda to follow them, hit a puddle of water, shook one paw in disgust, and fled back to the protection of the veranda. I watched my furry bedmate, wondered how Calico was getting on back in Friday Harbor, and began reading the report on Eric.

DataTech Confidential Report #11865420
Eric Arthur Szabo

DOB/POB:	February 5, 1965 at St. John's Hospital, San Francisco.
Parents/Siblings:	Arthur Szabo and Mary Castino, San Francisco; Patricia Szabo, Seattle
Current Address:	3690 Noe Street, San Francisco
SSN:	549-32-1500
Education:	B.A. in Philosophy, University of California, Santa Cruz, 1984, summa cum laude.
Marital Status:	1989, married Phyllis McArthur, Monterey, California. 1998, divorced from Phyllis McArthur, San Francisco County, no children.
Religion/Affiliation:	Buddhist; San Francisco Zen Center
Work History:	1988–1991 *Marin Independent Journal,* San Rafael, California; 1992–1996 *San Francisco Chronicle;* 1996–1998 Freelance photography for national magazines & wire services
	1997 Owner, Eric Szabo Photography, San Francisco (www.ericSzabophotography.com). Specializes in nudes, fashion, travel, food & wine.
Political Affiliation:	Registered Democrat
Club Memberships:	None
Professional Associations:	Professional Photographers of California; American Association of Media Photographers, Northern California Chapter; International Commercial Photographers Association.
Police Record:	December 31, 2001, Sausalito, California, D.U.I., found guilty; February 2002, reported theft of photographic equipment and negatives at 3690 Noe Street, San Francisco.
F.B.I. Record:	None
F.I.T. Taxes Due:	None
California Franchise Tax Board:	$6,760 unpaid taxes.
Credit Rating:	Unavailable

Automobile:	1991 Honda Odyssey, registration to Szabo Photography LLC

I began eating the banana bread, trying to compose a picture of Eric Szabo's life. He was smart and had achieved some degree of success in his field. He'd moved from a small-town newspaper to a metropolitan daily to national wire services, then to his own shop. It was impossible to tell from the background report how successful Eric Szabo Photography was and whether the unpaid debt to the California Franchise Tax Board was the result of lack of money or some dispute over amount owed. With no club memberships listed, it was difficult to visualize his social life. From what I remembered of alcohol consumption in San Francisco, the one D.U.I. was no surprise, particularly on December 31. I reread the specializations listed for Eric Szabo Photography, wondered what sort of bedmates—social or otherwise—a specialization of nude photography might have inspired, finished off the bread, and turned to Zoe's report.

DataTech Confidential Report #11865421
Zoe Rebecca Llewellyn

DOB/ROB:	Los Angeles, California; June 10, 1966
Parents/Siblings:	Roger Llewellyn and Leticia Gainesborough. Father former U.S. ambassador to Australia.
Education:	1985 Class valedictorian, Anna Head School, Oakland, CA.
	1989 Bachelor of Arts Degree in Radio/TV Broadcasting, U.C.L.A.

	1991, Master of Arts Degree in Journalism, U.C.L.A.
Marital Status:	Unmarried.
Religion/Affiliation:	Presbyterian. No current affiliation.
Profession/Career:	1989–91 Internship, KRSD Radio, San Diego

Profession/Career:
1989–91 Internship, KRSD Radio, San Diego
1992–98 Co-anchor, *News at Five,* Channel 9, Los Angeles
1998–2001 News anchor, *News at 10,* Channel 5, Tucson, Arizona
2001– Host, *Good Morning Santa Barbara,* KKSB. Suspended January 2003, pending resolution of a lawsuit filed against KKSB.

Awards:
1996 Received Los Angeles Area Emmy Award for *News at Five*

Political Affiliation:
Registered Democrat

Club Memberships:
Santa Barbara Tennis Club, Santa Barbara; Archangels of Lesbos

Professional Associations:
American Association of News Broadcasters; Santa Barbara Toastmasters Club

Police Record:
None

F.B.I. Record:
None

F.I.T. Taxes Due:
None

Lawsuits:
Co-defendant: Gonzales Bartholomew vs. KKSB, filed February 2003. Action pending.

Childhood Hobby:
Ice skating

Other:
June 2000 Received a California permit to carry a concealed weapon. October 10, 1999, *Tucson Daily Sentinel:* "Zoe Llewellyn, a morning news anchor at Tucson's Channel 5, has admitted to broadcasting information on her news show that contained quotes from people who said they never spoke with Llewellyn, and also contained factual errors. Ms. Llewellyn apologized for the inadvertent errors."

"See anything in the report that would motivate someone to push her off a cliff?" Zelda set down her plate and a glass of ice water across the table from me and took a seat.

I frowned, and watched Danielle and Joseph come into the dining room. They were followed a couple of seconds later by Andrea and Abigail. I handed Zelda the report and shook my head. "The picture I'm getting is of a smart, articulate newswoman who probably used her lesbian politics to push the envelope on a number of occasions. She's moved around a bit, but I think that's common for the profession."

Zelda scanned the report. "Did you know about the suspension from her TV show?"

"Yes. Danielle told me."

"She's got a permit to carry."

"She and several thousand other women in California."

"The Archangels of Lesbos sound a little over the edge," Zelda observed, handing back the report.

"The Archangels are a national group of militant lesbians. Most of the big cities have regional chapters. I think they call themselves a 'street-level direct-action group.' We had a case at the San Diego P.D. involving a woman who left her husband and went to live with her lesbian lover. Her husband found her and raped her. When the Archangels got done with him he wasn't very pretty."

"An eye for an eye?"

"Something like that, only the organ involved wasn't an eye."

"So what's all this got to do with falling off a

cliff on Santa Maria Island, fifteen hundred miles from Santa Barbara?"

I glanced at the report again and shook my head. "I don't think it does. There are only two ways on and off this island. By water or by air. The only plane that's been in here this week was the helicopter that took Eric to Bellingham. And there hasn't been a ferry since Tuesday, when everyone arrived. If somebody pushed Zoe off the cliff, it had to be a local. Murder is a pretty extreme measure to take to persuade your neighbors to move, but it's been done before. Did you and Mimi check all the rooms in the hotel?"

"I checked everything in this building, including the four rooms on this floor that haven't been renovated. Mimi and Graham checked all the outbuildings. Antonio followed the trail up to the cliff and checked where Zoe fell. He didn't see anything."

"Are you ready to take a drive?"

"Actually, boss, something's come up." She gave me a wide smile. Her green eyes were wide and guileless, which usually meant some sort of subterfuge was in the offing. "There's something I have to do this afternoon. These are the keys to the van. See you at dinner."

"There are two small tasks you could do before your afternoon engagement, if you would." I told her about the SSN mismatch for Antonio. "Find out who this Anthony Bustamante is. And this is the address for Tiffany's fiancé, Roberto Velásquez del Pino." I handed her the address and phone number I'd found in Tiffany's luggage. "See what you can get on him from DataTech, and find out who the phone number belongs to."

"Sure thing, boss." She laid a key ring with three keys beside my plate, gave me another smile, and headed toward the kitchen, her red ponytail bouncing with each step.

I watched her retreating back, puzzled by her recent secretive behavior, mystified by a lot of stuff that had occurred in the past three days, hopeful that I'd find Tiffany before she became the third "accidental" victim of Serenity and Light.

11

The seas below the hotel were foamed with whitecaps, but John Jordan had been right. There was less wind on the southeast side of the island. It was almost two o'clock by the time I left the hotel. The sun had come out and patches of blue sky were visible above rapidly moving dark clouds. Between the hotel and the Santa Maria General Store I met no pedestrians or other cars. I thought it unlikely that I'd find Tiffany sipping tea with Eloise Hausmann, but I stopped at the store anyway, parking the minivan alongside the pen of wild turkeys.

Eloise was alone in the store, ensconced on a stool behind the counter, smoking, watching a rerun of *The Golden Girls*. The white block letters on her fuchsia sweatshirt advised that "I don't have to attend every argument I'm invited to." She took my money for an Almond Joy bar without so much as a nod or any other indication that she'd ever seen me before in her life. There was no sign of Leroy, either his person or his old Harley.

Beyond the General Store the road curved sharply inland with small farms on both sides. Half a mile or so further on I came upon a woman in a dark red jacket and blue jeans walking along the left-hand side of the road. Her hair was long and dark brown, her shoulders stooped from the weight of the two canvas bags she carried. I pulled to a stop beside her and pressed the button that opened the window.

"Would you like a ride?"

The woman turned, hesitated, read the Dei Fiori decal on the side door of the van. She searched my face for a second or so, then nodded. "Sure. These bags are getting heavier by the minute."

She was younger than I'd judged by her stooped posture. Something about the face, with its sprinkling of freckles over the nose and the deep-set hazel eyes, suggested that she hadn't smiled in a long time.

"Where are you headed?" I asked.

"Over the hill, the second place on the right." She examined me with curiosity. "Are you the hotel owner?"

"My name's Scotia MacKinnon. I'm a guest at the hotel. I live in Friday Harbor."

"Donna Mulvaney." She pointed to a yellow house just over the crest. "That's it."

I stopped the van in front of a ramshackle house set under the spreading red branches of a huge madrona tree. Beyond the weathered barn a man in overalls was doing something to a split rail fence. The scene was pure Grant Wood. "That's Stuey," she said. "The sheep got out this morning." She climbed out of the van, pulling the two canvas bags with her. "Thanks for the ride."

"You're welcome. Incidentally, have you seen a tall blond woman around here today?"

She shook her head. "I saw a tall redhead up at the store yesterday. She was with John Jordan. Speaks English kind of funny. But no blonde." She was about to close the van door, then changed her mind. "You're the P.I., aren't you?" she asked.

"Excuse me?"

"I was at the store on Tuesday. A girl came in to buy milk. She told Eloise she was a maid at the hotel. She said one of the guests at the yoga retreat was a P.I. I figured it might be you. You have time for a cup of tea?"

The kitchen was warm and smelled of chocolate. The warmth came from the wood range across from the door, a cookstove like the one my grandmother Jessica had prepared our meals on in the big house in St. Ann's Bay. Donna had brewed our tea in a big white pot, pouring the water from the shiny metal teakettle that was simmering on the range.

I'd asked how long she and Stuey had lived on Santa Maria and learned that the Mulvaneys and Hausmanns had met in Alaska, where Stuey hadn't had any better luck with salmon fishing than Leroy. From there the two couples had gone to Colorado.

"Leroy's meaner than a snake." Donna took a long sip of her tea and her hazel eyes met mine over the cracked blue mug. "Stuey used to be a good man. Not a lot of brains, but he wasn't mean. Then he met Leroy and it was birds of a feather from then on. There's nothing Stuey wouldn't do for Leroy. And nothing Leroy wouldn't ask." She put the cup down on the red-checked oilcloth and wiped her mouth with her fingers. "Leroy says his name means 'the king' in French.

"We got run out of Colorado," she continued grimly, pouring herself another cup of tea. "Stuey and Leroy got drunk watching the Denver Broncos one Sunday. Then Leroy's stupid geese attacked the neighbor's dogs and when the dogs defended themselves, Stuey and Leroy beat the dogs so bad they had to be put down. They even gouged an eye out of the puppy." I shivered, suddenly cold, and she glanced toward the window. The slight man in overalls was bent over the fence. "I'd of left him, but the next week my daddy died and left this property to Stuey. Not to *Stuey and me*, but to *Stuey*." She shrugged. "It's a hundred acres and I didn't have anywhere else to go. So we moved back here. Stuey wants to raise sheep and Leroy started logging. Now he's run out of trees and I guess the only money's coming from the store."

"Eloise is the official postmistress?"

She nodded. "She's almost as mean as Leroy. Not quite, but almost. I hear there's been some trouble at the hotel," she said, changing the subject abruptly.

"There were a couple of accidents," I said quietly. "And one of the guests is missing."

"The photographer and the TV woman? Those weren't accidents," Donna said, biting her lower lip. "No way to prove it, but I'd bet my life on it."

"What do you mean?"

She leaned back in the chair and rubbed her neck. "It's no secret that Leroy got the whole island stirred up when he heard about the California woman buying the convent property and her plans for a hotel. What's her name, Mamie?"

"Mimi Rossellini," I said. "Her husband's name is Piero."

"Right. Mimi and Piero. Leroy was ranting and raving about a bunch of foreigners moving in and how life on Santa Maria was going to change and we'd be overrun with tourists and yachties and probably even have a ferry stopping here every day." She smiled for the first time. "Gee whiz, I thought we might even get telephones and electricity and start living in the twenty-first century, but Eloise almost had a coronary when I said so. Not that *that* would have been any great loss." She laughed mirthlessly. "But there's something else going on." Serious again, she groped for words, frowning, both hands wrapped around the blue mug. "Something . . . weird. Stuey gets more close-mouthed every day. Can't put my finger on what it might be."

"You mean something going on with Leroy or something having to do with the convent property? Or the hotel?"

"A girlfriend of mine in Friday Harbor works for one of the real estate agents. She told me Leroy put in a lowball offer on the property before Mimi bought it. When Leroy found out it'd been sold, he went roaring into the office like a madman, threatening to sue the agent."

"Do you know what he was going to do with the convent property?"

"I can't figure it out. He can't even pay the taxes on what he's got. Stuey almost jumped down my throat when I asked." She glanced toward the window again and stood up suddenly. "It'd be best if you went," she said quickly. "If Stuey sees your van with the hotel name on it, he'll tell Leroy, sure as shooting. I'd hate for anything more to happen over there."

It was 3:40 and I wanted to go by John Jordan's place, so I thanked her for the tea and pulled a business card and pen from my pocket. I wrote the hotel number on the card above my cell phone number. "If you learn anything more about Leroy's plans, call me," I said. "Or if you should see a tall blond woman." I glanced out the window, saw Stuey striding toward the barn. "And take care of yourself."

The yard was full of sunshine when I went out. Donna leaned out the door as I climbed into the van. "Tell Mimi to be careful of Leroy. He's a mean one. The whole family is. You hear about that incident over at Roche Harbor? Fracas between some college kids from the mainland and some locals? One of the kids got his ear cut off with a Swiss Army knife. That was Leroy's nephew did that."

Three miles beyond Donna and Stuey's place, in a grove of Douglas firs, I spied a bleached wooden sign with carved letters that said "Santa Maria Nubians." Tall lilac bushes hanging heavy with purple blooms lined both sides of the driveway to the red barn. I passed the small, weathered house and parked in front of the open sliding barn door. In the pasture to the right, four brown goats with long, floppy white ears strolled over to investigate me with soft eyes. I found John Jordan inside the barn, leaning over the top of a wooden stall. He smiled and motioned me to join him, and we gazed down at a tiny brown kid nursing from its mother.

"Born about an hour ago," he said proudly, hooking his fingers in the straps of his striped overall. "It's the third kid this week. Two more to go."

I glanced around. The barn looked a lot like the stable where Melissa had boarded a horse when she was ten, except this one smelled different. "What do you do with the little ones when they grow up?" I asked.

"I'm trying to build up a herd of breeder goats, so I keep the ones that look like they have potential and sell the others."

"You have to truck them to Friday Harbor and then over to the mainland, I presume?"

He nodded. "It's a bit of a hassle, particularly with only two ferries a week. It's not a popular idea with a lot of folks here, but I'd like to see the ferry service expanded. Then I'd be able to sell goat's milk. There's a market for it on the mainland. Tasha says her grandmother used to make goat cheese. She wants to try it here." He turned away from the stall and walked outside. "I presume you want to talk about the accidents. And Leroy. Have a seat over there if you like." He nodded at the metal tool chest against the barn wall and reached into a pocket for a pipe and an envelope of tobacco.

"Tell me about Leroy," I said, sitting down on the chest.

He filled the pipe, tamped down the tobacco, and lit it with a match that he extinguished by running it under an outside faucet. "Have you met Leroy?"

"I haven't been introduced, but I saw him at the store."

"Leroy is a piece of work," he began. "Everybody on Santa Maria is independent. Some of us, like me and Donna and Leroy, were born here and moved away and came back. Some came up the coast from California in the seventies and managed to eke out a living. We've got farmers and quilters and artists and writers. We've got McCarthy conservatives and people so far to the left they make Marx and Lenin sound like right-wingers. But until Leroy came back, everybody got along."

"I understand he got upset over someone's cash crop?"

John puffed on his pipe and nodded. "That someone was me and seventeen other residents. I wouldn't call it a cash crop. I had four plants, purely for my own enjoyment. I think there was one guy growing it for sale, somebody way up north of Gus's place. All the rest of us were just cultivating it for home use. Fortunately the sheriff's boys messed up and the case was dismissed or I'd be in jail right now. For something that ought to be legal anyhow. I don't think Leroy gave a damn what anybody was growing, but he's a shit-kicker, pure and simple."

"Leroy and some others signed a petition to keep the Rossellinis from opening the hotel," I said. "Was that on general principle or was there some other agenda?"

"Eloise was behind that. And up until a few months ago I would have said it was because most of the people live here because they want to be off the grid. They have their generators and their own wells. They don't care about telephones or computers or ferries. They want to do what they damn well please without anybody looking over their shoulders."

"But you have a telephone and a computer."

"I have a three-watt cell phone that works most of the time, and last fall I installed a little satellite dish that allows me to get an Internet connection. It cost an arm and a leg. My mother lives in Seattle and I need to be able to stay in touch with her." He smiled. "And if I hadn't, I wouldn't have found Tasha."

"So what happened a few months ago?"

"Almost a year ago, Leroy had some visitors. Six or eight city dudes. All dressed up in brand-new country clothes they just got from L.L. Bean. They were all over the island for a whole day. Then, in January, Leroy built a big wooden enclosure behind the general store. A few weeks later he was gone off-island for two weeks. When he came back, he had some animals in his truck. Whatever he's got, he keeps them locked up in the enclosed corral."

"What do you think he's up to? Buying and selling exotic animals?"

"Could be. He went and trapped a bunch of wild

turkeys over on San Juan. Said he was afraid the species was going to be extinct and he wanted to save them. What a hoot!"

There was the scrape of boot heels and Natasha joined us with a worried look on her face. "Oh, it's you, Scotia. I was coming to ask John to help me move the bedroom furniture and I saw the hotel car. I thought maybe it was Mimi. I don't have to go back to the hotel, do I?" Natasha moved over to John. He encircled her with one arm and dropped a kiss on her head.

"Not if you don't want to," I said. I glanced at the purple lilac bushes behind her, and the rolling green hills that rose beyond the pasture. "I think you made a great choice, Natasha. I came because Tiffany's still missing, and to see if John could shed any light on Eric or Zoe's accidents."

"Do you think the TV woman fell over the cliff by accident?" John asked.

"It's hard to say. What do you know about the Mulvaneys? Are they part of Leroy's shit-kicking crew?"

"You've met the Mulvaneys?" He gave me a sharp look. "Stuart Mulvaney fished up in Alaska until the fishery was depleted. That's where he met Leroy. I understand the four of them wound up in Colorado until they ran afoul of the law on an animal cruelty charge. They came back here right after Donna's dad died. Donna Mulvaney is a terrific woman. I understand she had a good job in Sitka when she met Stuart. Why she stays with that moron is beyond me. And I don't think there's a lot of love lost between Donna and Leroy. Incidentally, the day I found your boat line untied? Stuey was on the dock and did a quick disappearing act when I arrived."

I thought about what I wanted to do about that for a minute, then asked the sixty-four-dollar question. "Do you think Leroy's mean enough to attempt murder just to get Mimi and her husband off the island?"

John shrugged. "There was an incident back when we were growing up. A young girl from Bellingham was visiting her grandmother. She met Leroy at a beach party, and claimed he raped her and threatened to kill her if she told anyone. Leroy's father swore Leroy was home in bed when the rape supposedly happened. The girl had been drinking. There were no witnesses. The girl's family didn't have any money, so nobody pressed charges and Leroy left the island right after." He shrugged again. "Maybe that answers your question." He smiled at Natasha. "Shall we move that furniture now?"

I thanked John for his time, gave him my card, and headed for the van, enumerating what I'd learned about Leroy Hausmann and his family and their history of violence.

It was nearly four o'clock and there was one more Santa Maria resident who might know something about Tiffany. A thin plume of pale gray smoke drifted skyward from the chimney on Gus's stone stable. The sun had lost its battle to the dark storm clouds and the air was damp again with approaching rain. Gus's Golden Retriever tore down the grassy lane to the road in a frenzy of barking, then metamorphosed into a smiling Mr. Welcome Wagon as I got out of the van. I let him sniff my right hand, patted his silky head, and followed his wagging tail up to the stable, past the battered blue pickup parked in front. Gus stood above me at the top of the stone incline that was even with the second level of the structure. The door behind him was open.

"Afternoon." He put a hand on the Golden's head. "What can I help you with?"

"Good afternoon, Gus." I extended my hand, hoping he'd invite me inside. "I'm Scotia Mac-Kinnon. We haven't talked, but I'm staying at the hotel. I'm a private investigator. Mrs. Rossellini asked me to look into the accidents at the hotel this week."

"The photographer from San Francisco and the lady from Santa Barbara," he said, ignoring my outstretched hand.

"Yes. And now there is also a guest missing from the hotel. Tiffany Marr."

"She was at the hotel last night."

"I know. But she was gone this morning, and no one has seen her all day. There's no way for her to get off the island." A gust of wind whirled around us and a large raindrop fell on my nose. Gus continued to lean against the doorjamb with no indication of offering hospitality and little apparent concern for Tiffany's disappearance. With a growing sense of unease, I recalled Zelda's comment that Gus had a crush on Tiffany and called her "the lavender butterfly." Several more raindrops fell.

"Gus, would it be possible for me to come inside for a few minutes? I understand you've lived here a long time. Mimi thought perhaps you could help us find Tiffany or suggest where we might look."

Gus frowned and moved inside. I followed him and the Golden into the dim structure where the remains of a small fire burned in a stone fireplace. Two large and not terribly clean braided rugs covered the stone floor. Floor-to-ceiling bookshelves covered the wall to the right side of the fireplace. On the other side was a glass cabinet housing various components of a sound system. I noted that Gus also had a device that some locals used to amuse themselves by listening to their neighbors' cell phone calls.

Gus removed a long, dark garment from the scarred wooden rocking chair beside the hearth and motioned me to sit. He hung the garment on a hook near the door and leaned against the mantel over the hearth. "Lots of hiding places on Santa Maria if someone doesn't want to be found," he offered.

"Why do you think Tiffany wouldn't want to be found?"

He folded his arms over his chest and regarded me with unblinking blue eyes. "I have no idea, Ms. MacKinnon."

I was getting nowhere, but I plunged on anyway. "Last night I saw Ms. Marr talking to you at the hotel," I said. "Could you tell me what you were talking about? Did she give any indication that she might leave the hotel?"

"Ms. MacKinnon, I don't like being spied on." He regarded me silently for a long minute, blue eyes narrow. "She wanted to know about Mrs. Rossellini's plans for the new vineyard," he said grudgingly. "And she asked how to get up to the Butterfly Meadow. I didn't ask her why she wanted to go there." He looked away, took a poker from the galvanized pail beside the hearth, and turned the logs over so that the rosy embers faced up.

"Gus, I thought I saw you give Tiffany a small package last night. Could you tell me what was in the package?"

From somewhere on the lower floor a door crashed shut.

"Wind's coming up," Gus said. He glanced toward the door, still holding the poker. "You must have been mistaken about a package, Ms. MacKinnon, and you might want to be getting back to the hotel before it starts raining again. Sometimes we get a flash flood down the road a piece. It might be dangerous for you."

Ignoring Gus's suggestion—with its implied threat—and the lie about the package, I asked what he could tell me about Leroy Hausmann. Gus replaced the poker in the stand on the hearth, and sat down on a low bench near the fireplace. The Golden came and laid his head on Gus's knee.

"Before Leroy moved back to the island," he began, "people here had their differences, but they always worked them out without calling the sheriff. Then him and Eloise started stirring up trouble. First it was calling in the sheriff because some people was raising marijuana. Then it was the big fuss over turning the convent into a hotel. The marijuana fracas was because John Jordon objected to Leroy clear-cutting his 100 acres. Which he did anyway, then called the sheriff and reported that his neighbor was some kind of big-time drug lord."

"What was Leroy's objection to the hotel?"

"To hear him talk at the monthly community meeting, you'd think he was a lily-white environmentalist, all the B.S. he comes up with. Talks about keeping Santa Maria undeveloped and pristine. What I think is that Leroy wants the hotel for himself."

"He wants to run a *hotel*?"

Gus shrugged. "A fellow over in Friday Harbor told me Leroy put in a bid on the property after that woman from California was killed. I guess he thought her parents would just give it away. When he heard somebody bought it, he almost had a stroke. Maybe he wanted to log that land, too." He patted the golden's head, pulled the dog against his leg, then stood up and examined his watch. "I need to feed Sebastian his hay and put him inside before the storm gets any worse. You might want to be heading back. I hope you find Tiffany." He smiled and opened the door for me.

More than a little suspicious of Gus's nonchalance over Tiffany's disappearance, I watched him amble down toward the big black horse with its head over the corral gate, then I drove back the way I had arrived, over Mt. Houston, down Black Raven Road past Santa Maria Nubians and the Mulvaneys. I came to a stop beside the Santa Maria General Store. I was half tempted to confront Leroy, but the store was dark, the American flag whipping in the wind, the wild turkeys huddled together in their pen. If

Leroy had anything to do with the two accidents or Tiffany Marr's disappearance, bigger guns than I would be needed to take him on. Even if he had nothing to do with the accidents, a confrontation at this point might not be in Mimi's best interest. Some sleeping dogs should be let lie. Particularly dogs as mean as Leroy Hausmann.

12

"The red underwear didn't belong to Antonio," Zelda said. She followed me out of the dining room after Friday-night dinner, which had been even more somber than lunch. With Eric, Zoe, Natasha, and Tiffany gone, the group of retreat participants had diminished to three besides myself. Conversation was desultory and everyone but Abigail seemed to be looking over their shoulder. Nobody had heard anything from Tiffany, and there was no sign of Serafina or Mimi.

"So who does it belong to?" I pulled a message slip off the board, noting that it was from Nick and that he was going to call back.

"To Piero," she said ruefully, raising her eyebrows.

"To Piero!? Why on earth would he leave his underwear on . . . oh, no!"

"Oh, yes. Mimi confronted him. She also confronted him with this. It came in this afternoon. A colorful chap, our chef Piero."

She handed me a DataTech report and disappeared into Mimi's office. I leaned against the phone booth and scanned the report, wondering how many more blows to the emotional solar plexus Mimi could withstand.

DataTech Confidential Report #11865459
Matteo Piero Rossellini

POB/DOB:	Perugia, Italia; September 10, 1965
Parents/Siblings:	Piero Marcello Rossellini & Gina Donizetti Rossellini/no siblings
Citizenship:	Italy. Application for U.S. residency in process.
SSN:	None
Education:	Colegio di San Damiano, Asissi; Academia Culinaria di Roma
Marital Status:	Married Madeline Abbott St. Clair, June 10, 2002, Sorrento, Italy
Religion/Affiliation:	Catholic. No current affiliation.
Profession/Career:	Ristorante San Gimignano; Ristorante La barca, Firenze; San Vicenzo Ristorante; Albergo Ristorante di San Lorenzo, Cofino.
Political Affiliation:	Unknown
Club Memberships:	Club Tennis Costa Amalfi
Professional Associations:	Associazione Culinaria d'Italia
Police Record:	None on record (see below).
F.I.T. Taxes Due:	No record of F.I.T. taxes paid.
Lawsuits:	March 15, 1997 Named as corespondent in a divorce suit instituted by Professor Carlo Luigi Di Paoli against his wife, Leda Maria da Ponte.
Other:	*Il Corriere de la notte, Genti* September 10, *2000*: "For the third time this month Mrs. Sofia Cerement, wife of one of Florence's city council members, was seen on the arm of her favorite chef, Matteo "Piero" Rossellini, at the opening

performance of Prokofiev's *The Love for Three Oranges*. This reporter wonders if there is more to the friendship than culinary interest." *(DataTech translation)*

Il tempo (Rome). February 5, 2001: "The police from Rome's 871st precinct were called to the Ristorante Tres Campanas on Vicolo della Campana to quell an altercation that arose shortly before midnight. According to witnesses, the encounter began when Tomasso Fallarino of Palermo approached the table where Matteo "Piero" Rossellini was dining with two friends. Mr. Fallarino reportedly threw a glass of red wine into Mr. Rossellini's face and challenged him to a duel for trifling with his wife. Mr. Rossellini's two friends then assaulted Mr. Fallarino, who was immediately defended by his two bodyguards. Mr. Fallarino's name has been linked to la Cosa Nostra and he was believed to be behind the 1998 bombing in Palermo which killed 34 people. *(DataTech translation)*

Zelda came out of Mimi's office and locked the door as I finished reading the translations of the newspaper articles at the bottom of the report.

"*Don Giovanni* in the flesh," she said impishly. "His life sounds like an Italian opera."

"What's Mimi going to do?"

"She marched into the kitchen, threw the red bikinis and a copy of the report in Piero's face and disappeared into her bedroom. Maybe she's going to fire him like she did Rita."

"Easier said then done, I would imagine. I don't

suppose she reported Tiffany's disappearance to the sheriff?"

"Not yet." Zelda checked her watch and yawned. "I think I'll take a shower and go to bed early. You going on the wildflower walk tomorrow morning?"

"What wildflower walk?"

She nodded toward the message board. "Graham says there's going to be a window of good weather tomorrow morning before the next front comes in. He's offered to take everybody up to the meadow for a little excursion. I guess he used to be a botany teacher."

"I'll take it under consideration. If Mimi comes out of seclusion, I'd like to talk to her. What did you find out from Antonio about the phony SSN?"

"He says he decided to Italianize his name on the application because Mimi's ad on the Internet asked for Italian speakers. And the reason he's been so glum is that his girlfriend in L.A. is mad at him because he has a hard time calling her from here. Apparently, if Mimi wants to replace Rita, the girlfriend would be happy to come up for the summer."

"Might not be a bad idea." I frowned, still bothered by my conversation with Gus. There was also something I'd read in the original background report on him that was nagging me, but I couldn't remember what it was. I slid into the phone booth and dialed Nick's number, got his voice recording. Increasingly apprehensive about our relationship, worried about Tiffany, and suspicious of Gus, I headed off to my own room.

*   *   *

I found the item on Gus's background report that had worried me: His stepdaughter had disappeared when she was fourteen. The family was living on the Kitsap Peninsula at the time, west of Seattle. There was nothing in the report to indicate whether the girl had ever been found. Three years later he'd been divorced from the girl's mother. I stared at the printed words for a long time, then undressed and crawled into bed with Mao. I was dozing over *The Girl in the Plain Brown Wrapper* a little after ten o'clock when I heard a soft knock on my door. None of the doors had a spy hole, but since Natasha had moved out, the visitor was probably either Mimi or Zelda.

It was, in fact, Andrea who stood outside the door, long bare feet in a pair of leather thong sandals, a gold polar fleece shirt over a pair of faded blue jeans, an anxious smile on her tanned, high-cheekboned face. She took in my freshly scrubbed face and the pajamas.

"Scotia, I'm sorry to disturb you so late. It's just that I was worried about Tiffany. I could not sleep. Zelda told me you were searching for Tiffany today. May I come in?"

Reluctantly, I motioned her inside, not wanting to discuss the results of my afternoon with anyone but Mimi. Mao gave me a dirty look and leaped for the open window. I removed a pile of clothes from the wooden chair in front of the desk and Andrea sat down, curling one leg under her, putting both hands in the pockets of her fleece jacket.

"Did you find out anything about Tiffany?"

"Not really," I said. "When was the last time you saw her?"

She frowned. "Saw her? Dinner on Wednesday? I think she was at yesterday's afternoon session with Joseph. She was not at dinner last night. I was worried about her. I knocked on her door last night, but she was not there."

"What time was that?"

"Maybe nine o'clock." Her black eyes widened. "Do you think her being missing has anything to do with Zoe's death?"

"It's hard to say at this point." Recalling that DataTech had come up with nothing on an Andrea M. Cross from Los Angeles, I reached for my tape recorder. "Mimi asked for my help in looking into Zoe's accident, so I've been talking to the guests and staff. Since you're here, would you mind answering a few questions?"

She glanced at the tape recorder. "What kind of questions?"

"Just boilerplate stuff for the record in case the sheriff or anyone needs to follow up."

She shrugged, pushed her hands deeper into her pockets, and produced a small smile. "Sure."

"Your full name is . . . ?"

"Andrea Margarita Cross."

"Have you ever used any other name?"

More wide black eyes and a shake of her head.

"Address and phone number?"

She supplied a street address and zip code for Los Angeles. It was the same address she'd put on her hotel registration.

"Place of birth?"

A slight hesitation, then, "Mexico."

"How long have you lived in this country?"

Another hesitation, then, "Seven years."

"Your English is very good."

She smiled. "I studied it in . . . before I came here.

"Marital status?"

"Single."

"Children?"

She blinked and shook her head.

"How did you find out about the retreat?"

She frowned. "Why are you asking?"

"Just a routine question," I said with a smile. "Mimi was wondering how effective her advertising was."

"A friend told me about it."

"What is your occupation?"

She combed her hair back with her fingers before answering. As she lifted her arm, I glimpsed a tattoo on the inside of her elbow. It looked like a tiny black panther. "Social worker," she replied.

"County or state agency?"

"It is a private agency," she said. She unfolded her leg and sat up straight in the chair, crossed one knee over the other. The smile had disappeared and she was watching my face warily. "We work with homeless women." She stood up and moved toward the door. "I am sorry to bother you. I hope you find Tiffany." She opened the door and glanced briefly back over her shoulder before leaving.

I played back my recorded conversation with Andrea, then lay on the bed and stared for a long time at the carvings on the inside of my wooden door, pondering why my questions to Andrea about her work had made her turn defensive, trying to zero in on exactly what about her seemed not quite . . . in sync.

Almost without exception, everyone has something they want to hide, and the kinds of things that people get defensive about may or may not be related to anything you want to know. As I speculated on why Andrea was using a false name and address, I remembered that a friend who is a Sherlock Holmes buff has more than once reminded me, "The more bizarre a thing is, the less mysterious it proves to be." So Andrea's secrets might have nothing at all to do with Eric or Zoe or Tiffany. Then again, they might.

Sleepless now, I typed up summaries of my conversations with Danielle and Andrea, and summarized my activities of the afternoon. Reading over the Danielle portion, I underlined her comment about the "something sensational" that Zoe had been working on when she was killed, and realized that in the confusion of Tiffany's disappearance this morning I hadn't called Zoe's supervisor in Santa Barbara to ask her about Zoe's "gangs in L.A." story. I also realized I hadn't asked Danielle if Zoe had brought a laptop with her. Ruefully I looked over my list of things to do, which included learning more about Andrea, calling the Santa Barbara TV station, and trying to get hold of Eric one more time. I would never make it to tomorrow morning's wildflower walk. I climbed into bed and put out the light, cranky and frustrated at having my vacation disrupted, plagued by the realization that there had been one unpleasant incident every day since I'd arrived at the hotel. Would there be another one tomorrow?

At one A.M., still sleepless, staring into the darkness, I shifted the Hotel Dei Fiori puzzle into the back of my brain and thought about Melissa and Simon and me. I especially thought about Melissa's accusation that if I'd accompanied Simon on his dive expedition to the Seychelles, there wouldn't have been a divorce and we would have all been together. She might have been right. But I know only too well that there's no returning to a road not taken, and at two o'clock I put on the light to read. As if waiting for a signal that it was clear to return, Mao leaped to the bed from the window to track muddy paw prints across the comforter. I towel-dried his paws and damp fur, and stroked his strong, sinewy body. When he curled into a ball near my pillow, I decided to take a walk.

The silent corridor was lighted by two antique bronze ceiling fixtures, at either end. Only Graham's door had a crack of light under it. I wondered what was keeping the professor awake.

In the great room, the heavy furniture cast long shadows on the floor and walls in the reflected glow of the dying fire. I hesitated before opening the door that led to the courtyard, thinking I saw a moving figure and a flash of light. Outside, the wind was cool. I let the heavy door swing shut behind me, hoping it would open from the outside when I returned. The flash of light had come from the hot tub area, where I could see clouds of steam and hear the muted roar of the spa jets. I also heard Zelda's giggle. Amused at her choice of hours for hot-tubbing, wondering who she was with, I approached the redwood tub that had been sunk several feet into the corner of the courtyard. Two arms, one male, one female, arose from the steam in greeting.

"*Bon soir, madame*. Are you going to join us?" The voice was low and male and carried an unmistakable French accent.

I peered into the steam, suddenly understanding my assistant's recent penchant for retiring early. "*Jean Pierre*?"

The darker head nodded. "*Oui, madame*. It is a pleasure to see you again."

Jean Pierre Zola was skipper on a large luxury yacht from Seattle that frequently moored at Roche Harbor. He had come into Zelda's life in conjunction with a previous case and at one time had invited her to go to Alaska with him.

Zelda's head emerged from the steam. "I smuggled him in," she offered gratuitously. "Please don't tell Mimi."

"At this point, it's purely academic, isn't it?"

"You're probably right. Incidentally, boss, I've decided I'm taking off for Alaska next week." She smiled and bussed Jean Pierre on the cheek. "We'll be back in July."

I looked from one beaming face to the other and offered my congratulations. Jean Pierre moved a few inches closer to Zelda. "Scotia, there's room if you want to join us."

I glanced at the swirling water, assumed that the two were *au naturel*, and decided that under the circumstances three would be an odd number. "I'm heading back to bed. And just on general principle, you might want to skedaddle before daylight."

"Yeah, you're right. By the by, I forgot to mention that while you were out sleuthing this afternoon, Mimi had an interesting visitor. Some contractor with plans for a cell phone tower."

"On Santa Maria?"

"Not only on Santa Maria, but on this very property. He had a signed lease dated a week before Mimi made her offer on the property. The cell company paid a ten-thousand-dollar deposit on a fifty-year lease to put a tower in the Butterfly Meadow."

I shook my head in amazement. "Who signed the lease?"

"The signature is illegible, but it was for Santa Maria Safaris. The contractor accused Mimi of changing the name on the property and said he's going to sue her if she doesn't honor the contract."

I bade the lovers good-night and returned to my room, pondering the matter of the lease, virtually certain that Santa Maria Safaris was Leroy Hausmann, incredulous that Leroy could have negotiated a signed lease without producing evidence that he owned the property. I was even more certain that Leroy was the instigator not only of the malicious mischief that had plagued Mimi's renovation, but of the far more serious accidents of the past week. Having received a deposit from the cell company and signed a lease for the cell tower, he certainly had a motive for chasing Mimi away. While the cell company had no legal right to the property, it could cost Mimi a lot of money in legal fees to clarify the issue.

When I turned on the light in my room, Mao put one paw over his eyes and went on snoozing. My mind a muddle, at four thirty I fell into an exhausted sleep and dreamed that Nick and his exwife Cathy were running across the Butterfly Meadow and I was pursuing them with a Japanese sword.

13

Saturday morning dawned with a red sky so brilliant behind dramatic dark clouds that any sailor within a hundred miles would surely have taken warning. Breakfast, despite the rosy baked apples stuffed with cinnamon granola and topped with fresh whipped cream, was even grimmer than dinner the night before. I learned from Zelda that Danielle had decided not to leave on the ferry and I wondered why she'd changed her mind.

I waited outside the dining room until Mimi came upstairs. She looked terrible, with dark circles under puffy eyes, wearing a shapeless white sweater over a long, wrinkled, blue cotton skirt. I flinched inwardly, regretting the pain I'd caused her by discovering the red underwear on *Gray Mist*. Why the hell hadn't I left the stupid red bikinis where I found them? Or better yet, gotten rid of them? She drew me into the office and closed the door.

"Zelda says you wanted to talk to me." She sat

at her cluttered desk and clasped her hands together on the desktop.

I handed her the typed report on my previous days' activities and my conversations with Danielle and Andrea, then verbally summarized my conclusions.

"The consensus among Donna Mulvaney, John Jordan, and Gus is that Leroy Hausmann is a mean, conniving troublemaker who's certainly capable of dirty tricks and possibly capable of murder if he thought he could get away with it. Nobody outside the hotel has seen Tiffany. You need to call the sheriff and report her disappearance," I said. "Or I'll do it if you like."

"Would you, Scotia?" She said it listlessly and pushed the phone toward me.

I dialed the sheriff's office, got Jeffrey Fountain, the undersheriff, and told him Mimi wanted to report a hotel guest missing on Santa Maria.

"A missing woman? What the Sam Hill is going on over there, Scotia? A photographer falls down the stairs, a TV talk-show host tumbles off a cliff, and now a woman's disappeared. And I'm sitting here staring at a box of audio cassettes that just came in from some kook on Santa Maria who says he thinks a bunch of South Americans are planning an assassination! For Chrissake, has everybody on Santa Maria gone *bananas*? Anyway," he said with a loud sigh of resignation, "give me the details."

Watching Mimi's face, I described the details of Tiffany's disappearance, including her fear of her fiancé.

"I'll see if I can get one of the deputies over there this morning," he promised.

"Is anyone going to do an investigation into Zoe Llewellyn's death?" I asked.

"It's been marked 'accidental.' No evidence of foul play, unless you know something we don't."

"Does the name Leroy Hausmann ring any bells, Jeff?"

"It rings lots of bells, Scotia, but what's a shit-kicker like Leroy got to do with a yoga retreat at the . . . the Dei Fiori Hotel? Are you suggesting he had something to do with the accidents?"

"I talked to a few of the locals and I've been hearing that Leroy had his eye on the convent property before the Rossellinis bought it. And not only had his eye on it, but signed a lease for a cell company to put a cell tower on it."

"That sounds like a civil matter Mrs. Rosselini should talk to her lawyer about. If you expect Nigel to get the department involved, you'll have to come up with something concrete, like an eyewitness to the accidents. So keep us posted."

I put the handset back in the cradle, knowing from past experience that it would take evidence so blatant it was hitting him in the face before Sheriff Nigel Bishop would admit that a crime had been committed in San Juan County.

"I should have asked the undersheriff to talk to the guests when Zoe got killed, shouldn't I?" Mimi said wearily. "I don't seem to be doing anything right these days. Not with the hotel and not with my personal life."

"Don't beat up on yourself, Mimi," I said gently.

"After Carl left me for a younger woman, I felt absolutely rotten. That's why I went to Italy. Staying at the convent helped. Then I met Piero. He was so gorgeous and affectionate. He made me feel like a teenager. When I first met him, I told him the difference in our ages was too much, but he said it didn't matter. He said I was easy to talk to, and so much fun to be with, so creative, and he would love me forever. How could I have believed it would work? And for him to come on to a child like Rita!"

"The 'coming on' was probably not just one-sided, Mimi."

"It doesn't matter now. Everything's turning into a nightmare. What are we going to do about Tiffany? How are we going to find her?"

"I've got some leads to follow up, and depending on who goes on the wildflower walk this morning, there's something I want to check out if you could loan me the master key to the west wing once more. It's a long shot, but who knows?"

She shook her head, reached into the desk drawer, and pulled out the large brass key. "Good luck to both of us. I sure could use some."

The wildflower group—Joseph, Graham, Abigail, Danielle, and Andrea—departed a little after ten, cameras over shoulders, rain gear in backpacks in the event that the "window of sun" Graham had predicted closed before they returned. From my room, I watched them file across the courtyard and disappear behind the hotel, where they'd pick up the steep path to the Butterfly Meadow and on to the fateful overlook. I waited ten minutes, checked the corridor, left my door ajar, walked to Andrea's room at the farthest end of the east wing. I closed the door and locked it from the inside with the dead bolt, praying she wouldn't change her mind about the excursion. If she returned early, my only means of retreat would be through the window, which was the same type as the one Tiffany had climbed or been carried through.

At first glance, I thought that Andrea's room had been ransacked. At second glance, I realized that the woman was simply a slob. Like one of Melissa's former college roommates, she apparently left each item of clothing where it fell when she removed it.

A pair of designer blue jeans lay strewn across the desk, partially covering a photograph in an ornate silver frame. Colored cotton shirts cluttered the bottom of the closet, tangled with pink satin bras and matching French-cut panties. The shirts were clean and must have been snatched from the hangers in haste or frustration. The flowered black skirt she'd worn to dinner the night before hadn't made it any further than the floor at the foot of the bed. Yesterday's yoga attire, a turquoise leotard and pull-on black stretch capris, were draped over an open bureau drawer. On the top of the bureau, an uncapped tube of Colgate toothpaste accompanied a large plastic container of eye makeup.

Resisting the impulse to start organizing, I moved over to the black-and-brown leather suitcase on the luggage rack beside the closet, rummaged through the contents, found a lot of clean and dirty girl attire. The side pockets yielded up a box of tampons, a small satin case of gold jewelry, and a gold cigarette lighter. The luggage carried no identification tag and no monogram. I checked the outside zippered pocket of the suitcase and found a thin, tan leather purse, which in turn contained a thin matching tan leather wallet with two credit cards, a small color photograph of a teenaged boy, and a California driver's license. The two credit cards, a health insurance card, and the driver's license were all issued in the name of Andrea Marta de la Cruz. The address shown on the four documents was San Diego, California. I examined the image on the driver's license. Andrea's hair had been shorter when the photo was taken, but it was unmistakably her. I replaced the wallet in the purse and put it back where I'd found it.

The photograph in the silver frame showed a dark-haired man of medium height squatting on a beach in a bathing suit. One arm was draped around the shoulders of a young boy. The woman with them was a smiling, younger version of Andrea. I leaned closer and examined the man again. He was slightly taller than Andrea. The face was handsome with no easily recognizable ethnicity. The face looked vaguely familiar. I didn't recognize the beach and there were no figures in the background. Andrea had said she'd never been married, which might or might not be true. She'd also said she had no children. Any assumptions I might make about the two people with her in the photo could be wildly inaccurate and misleading. The child might be the man's son. The man could be a lover or a husband or a brother or cousin. Or a stranger she met on the beach.

Underneath the blue jeans on the desk I discovered a shiny black-and-silver laptop computer. A telephone-modem connector dangled off the side of the desk, as useless as mine had proven to be. I checked my watch. It was 10:56 and the group wasn't expected back until lunchtime. I opened the cover of the laptop, pressed the power button, waited while Windows filled the screen and loaded its icons along the bottom.

At the other end of the corridor the outside door opened and closed. I glanced at the dead bolt and then at the window. Ear to the door, I heard movement farther down the corridor. No key was inserted in the door, and a minute or so later I heard the outside door open and close again. Whoever it was did not appear in the courtyard and I began to check out the contents of Andrea Marta de la Cruz's computer files.

Half an hour later, I'd found fifteen or twenty data files in her Word program, but all were password-protected. With enough time, Zelda might be able to breach the passwords, but I didn't dare take the computer. It was 11:30 and I had to get out of there. I shut down the laptop, wiped my fingerprints from the keyboard and outside cover with a pair of sweat socks, and gave a last glance around the room, noticing for the first time the tan leather portfolio almost hidden by the flowered duvet on the bed. The portfolio was unzipped and inside I found a letter written in black ink dated the tenth of the previous month. It was written on thin paper in Spanish. There was no envelope.

My second husband was Mexican American and my understanding of spoken Spanish is better than of written Spanish, but the language in the letter was simple and I understood from the closing that the writer was Andrea's mother. She described a family dinner, two new grandchildren, the worsening political situation with three kidnapings in the capital, said that "Carlitos" missed her, and closed with the hope that she would see Andrea soon. There was no address on the letter and the political conditions it mentioned could have been those in any one of half a dozen Latin-American republics.

I was baffled by what I'd found in the room and why Andrea had lied about her name and address. Wondering if any of it was important to my investigation for Mimi, I glanced out the window at the first of the wildflower group filing back into the courtyard. Graham and Abigail headed for the door at the far end of the west wing, while Andrea and Danielle moved toward the entrance to the great room around the corner from Andrea's room. I opened the dead bolt quietly, stepped outside, locked up, power-walked to my room at the end of the corridor, and slipped inside.

Heading up to the dining room for Saturday lunch, I realized that it was Nick's daughter's wedding day. The wedding was scheduled for one o'clock. I wondered what Nicole's wedding dress looked like, whether she was carrying white roses, what color her bridesmaid dresses were. I tried, not for the first time, to identify the source of her ongoing animosity toward me. Although I had met Nick in San Francisco when he was still married to Cathy, I was in no way responsible for their breakup. That had come after Cathy fell in love with her financial counselor. It was several years after that before Nick and I got together again. As I headed for Mimi's office, for a few brief seconds I visualized how beautiful Nick would look in a tuxedo. And I wished with all my heart that I was the one sitting beside him during the ceremony.

Mimi's office door was open. She'd styled her hair and put on makeup, changed into black silk trousers and a royal blue mandarin jacket. She gave me a questioning look when I returned the master key. I described the name and address discrepancies I'd discovered about Andrea and explained that I needed access to the Internet to determine if the discrepancies had anything to do with the trouble at the hotel. Mimi promised the use of her computer after lunch and I joined the group in the dining room in time to catch the full force of Abigail's wrath against the "miscreant that kidnaped our wild turkeys."

From what I could piece together, the trail up to the Butterfly Meadow had been too muddy and Danielle had not wanted to return to the scene of Zoe's death, so Graham had taken the group in the other direction, past the General Store and up to Black Raven Road, where the Nootka roses were blooming in profusion. Passing the General Store, Abigail had discovered the penned-up wildfowl, which apparently hadn't received their morning ration of grain. One of the wild turkeys in particular had caught her eye.

"It was Dorothy, I'd swear it. I saved that little chick when those horrible Basset boys were tormenting it two years ago. And she remembered me!"

Abigail had charged into the store to inquire as to the provenance of the turkeys and received a less-than-amiable welcome from a large woman who suggested that Abigail make fast tracks off her property and not come back. "She wouldn't tell me her name or who stole the turkeys."

"The store owners are Eloise and Leroy Hausmann," I offered.

Abigail wrote the names on her paper napkin and slid her chair back. "Well, folks," she said grimly, "I'm going to have a little talk with my nephew who works for Fish and Wildlife. Eloise and Leroy may be in for a little surprise."

I watched her march out of the dining room in her blue denim overalls, long white braid bouncing against her shoulder, and suddenly I had something else to worry about. What might happen to Abigail if Leroy discovered yet another female was standing in his way?

Mimi turned her office over to me after lunch. My first call was to Santa Barbara information and then to Janet Larson, the Program Director at KKSB, who was in a meeting. When I told her assistant I was investigating the death of Zoe Llewellyn, I heard a sharp intake of breath and Ms. Larson was immediately available.

"Was it really an accident?" she asked. "Her falling off the cliff? People here are speculating that she got involved in something she shouldn't have. And I was hoping her going up to the San Juans would be good for her."

"According to the San Juan County medical examiner, the cause of death was two blows to the head with a sharp object," I said. "That could have been the rocks she fell onto at the base of the cliff. I've been hired by the innkeeper here at the Hotel Dei Fiori on Santa Maria Island to look into the accident. I understand Zoe was on suspension. Could you tell me about that?"

Janet Larson sighed. "We had no choice. I felt bad about it. Zoe had great potential. If she'd given me the slightest hint that she planned to out that poor old man, I would have talked her out of it. She couldn't have chosen a worse subject for her crusade. For Christ's sake, everybody knows Bartholomew is gay, but he's a pillar of the community—involved in all the little theater productions, donates stacks of money every year to the art foundation—and nobody gives a damn who he sleeps with."

"I understand Mr. Bartholomew filed a suit against your station?"

"The very next day. He's asking for fifty million dollars. Our attorneys are in a dither and don't know how they're going to get out of it. Not that he'll ever get fifty million, but even half or a quarter of that could ruin us."

"Did Zoe or the station get any threatening calls after Bartholomew's appearance?"

"Any *calls*?! Our switchboard was jammed for three days. I don't know that any *threats* were made against Zoe, but the Santa Barbara upper crust was furious. And, of course, there were also calls in her support. From her pals at Archangels of Lesbos, my assistant said. *They* threatened to close down the station if Zoe's suspension wasn't lifted."

"Did Zoe have any close personal friends at the station?"

"No, I don't think so. I never saw her socializing with anyone."

"Did you know her partner, Danielle?"

"I met her once."

"Could you describe Zoe's relationship with Danielle?"

"I'd prefer not to discuss Zoe's personal life." Her voice turned cool. "And I do have a meeting in ten minutes."

"Of course. Just one more question: Could you tell me what project or feature Zoe was working on at the time of her suspension? Something she was into that might have offended someone?"

I listened to dead air for several seconds. "There was one story she wanted to do. She turned in a draft to me just before the suspension." More dead air. "It had something to do with gangs. I didn't think it was appropriate for us and decided not to run it. If it's really important, I could fax a copy of the outline to you."

"I'd appreciate that." I gave her the hotel fax number, thanked her for her time. I hung up and stared at my notes, nonplussed, unable to imagine any connection between a feature story on gangs and Zoe's death on Santa Maria. The office was growing dim. I glanced out the window at the darkening clouds. Our window of good weather was already history.

I turned on the office light and checked for e-mail, found a message from Melissa advising that she'd given the Dei Fiori number to Simon, who wanted to come to Friday Harbor and see me next week. There was also a message from Michael Farraday, brief as usual, though not as cryptic as some previous ones.

Dinner at the Empress on May 28? I'll have a plane and can pick you up in Friday Harbor. Please say yes. I need your help.

So Michael Farraday was a pilot. I remembered the disappearing act he and his F.B.I. buddy had done last summer when the only clue as to how they'd gotten off Lopez Island was the report of a woman who'd seen a float plane take off from Mackay Harbor. As for an agent with British Military Intelligence needing the help of a small-town P.I., it wasn't likely. And yet . . .

I checked Mimi's calendar. May 28 was next Tuesday. If Nick came through with his proposed plan to take a vacation after the wedding, the date wouldn't work. The wedding would be over today. Nick was sure to call tomorrow. I would wait before replying.

There was a third message from the private investigator in Trinidad, who advised she would be happy to track down Mr. Petrovsky when he arrived and present whatever documents we wanted to send. I forwarded the message to Friday Harbor attorney Carolyn Smith.

I had one more task before logging off. I clicked up the DataTech web site, entered my password, requested an in-depth background check on Andrea Marta de la Cruz, with the San Diego address I'd found on her driver's license. I was about to close up the office when the phone rang. The caller was Donna Mulvaney.

"I called to ask if the woman you were looking for showed up . . . Tiffany somebody?"

"Tiffany Marr. No, she hasn't. Do you have information about her?"

"No, but I've been thinking about what we talked about, the accidents and all. The more I think about it and the way Stuey's been acting lately, the more I'm positive Leroy's behind all the trouble at the hotel. It's hard to tell if he's doing it out of pure meanness or if he's got something up his sleeve, but maybe tonight you could find out. I'm worried about Stuey. I think he's in over his head."

"What's happening tonight?"

"Every Saturday night Stuey and Leroy and our other neighbor, Homer Black, head up-island to a poker game. They take off on their bikes around about seven o'clock, don't come roaring back until almost midnight. I thought, since you're a private detective, you could find a way to get into Leroy's office at the store and maybe figure out what's going on."

I glanced out the window to the hill behind the hotel, where a fine mist of rain was falling, and considered the feasibility of what Donna was proposing. While my priority was to find Tiffany, if Leroy was involved in the accidents or some scheme to get Mimi out of the hotel, there might well be evidence in his office.

"Donna, do you have any specific reason to think Leroy might be responsible for Tiffany's disappearance?"

"Not exactly, except I was at the store this morning and heard Eloise and Leroy joking about a call Leroy got from his nephew's wife that works in the sheriff's office. I guess you guys must've filed a missing persons' report. Leroy thought that was the funniest thing he'd ever heard."

I hesitated, reflecting on the professional ethics of the sheriff's staff. "I'd go with you," Donna said, "but if anything went wrong . . . well, I have to live here."

"What about Eloise? Where will she be tonight?"

"She usually goes over to Mabel Black's after dinner on Saturday and they drink a big bottle of red wine and watch *I Love Lucy* reruns. She's usually there until at least ten. I can see the Black's house easy from here."

"What time will she be going to Mabel's?"

"Between seven and eight."

"Does the store have an alarm system?"

"I don't think so. Leroy's too cheap."

"Any dogs?"

"Not anymore. Leroy had one, but it made so much noise barking at the turkeys, he gave it to somebody over in Friday Harbor." She giggled. "And maybe while you're there, you could find out what kind of strange animals Leroy's got behind that tall fence."

"How's the cell phone reception at the store?"

"It's pretty good there about ninety percent of the time. Give me your cell phone number again. If any of them come home early, I can warn you."

I thanked her and hung up the phone, already making a mental list of the items I'd need to break into Leroy's office, all of which were on *DragonSpray*.

I had no idea if Mimi and Piero had come to some sort of accommodation regarding his peccadilloes, or were even on speaking terms. Dinner was *filetti di pesce con broccoli* and was served on time. Joseph and Graham sat by themselves at the round table in the corner window. Mimi sat next to me and reported *sotto voce* that various items of food had disappeared from the kitchen that afternoon, including a loaf of banana bread and a whole cooked chicken. No one could account for the two towels that had disappeared from the bathroom in the west wing, and Andrea had reported her cell phone missing from her room. I couldn't imagine how Andrea could have possibly noticed anything was missing from her pigsty of a room. Recalling the midnight tryst in the hot tub I'd interrupted the night before, I glanced across the table at Zelda, who was whispering with Abigail, and wondered if the missing food had been smuggled to her visiting French skipper.

Only half listening to Mimi's conjecture that the spiteful Rita had probably filled up her suitcase before she left for parts unknown, I finished the halibut and watched Antonio gathering up the dirty dishes, speculating on the possibility that the young man who'd Italianized his name could be one of Roberto's goons. While I didn't dismiss the idea completely, the fact that Antonio had offered to bring up his girlfriend to replace Rita made it seem far-fetched.

*   *   *

The earlier mist had turned to a light drizzle at seven fifteen when I slipped out of the hotel. I'd checked the message board when I left the dining room after dinner. Mimi was working in her office and there was only one new message on the board with my name on it. It was from Simon; the message was that his trip to Friday Harbor would be delayed. He'd call back. I breathed a sigh of relief and headed down to the marina, recalling that I hadn't responded to Falcon's latest invitation.

I wondered again what Nick was doing. The wedding reception would have been over by six or so. Was he sitting around with friends and family? Shoring up Cathy after having married off their only daughter? Trying to make reservations for our getaway?

The tools I needed for breaking and entering Leroy's office were in a locker in *DragonSpray*'s aft cabin. I assembled a flashlight, lock picks, surgical gloves, and my digital camera. In the hanging wardrobe in the aft cabin, I found a dark sweater and sweat pants, and exchanged the yellow foul-weather jacket for an old dark blue slicker. Remembering Donna's characterization of Leroy as "meaner than a snake," I retrieved my Beretta from the tiny hidden locker in the main cabin, checked the safety, found extra ammo, and as an afterthought, added a stun gun to other tools in the black rucksack. I pulled on a pair of black sailing boots, checked the water level on both batteries, and locked up the boat.

Next stop: the Santa Maria General Store.

14

It was 8:25 when I got to the store. The lock on the entrance door was pretty much a piece of cake, primarily because whoever had left the store last had forgotten to turn the dead bolt. The only light inside was a low-wattage bulb above the cash register that left the grocery area in darkness. A woman's red cloth purse lay on the counter beside the cooler. I glanced toward the post office at the back of the store and studied the closed door to Leroy's office, listening for any sound that would indicate Eloise hadn't left yet. After a couple of minutes, I slid the purse out of the light and used my flashlight to check the contents, which included a wallet with a Washington driver's license issued to Eloise Hazel Hausmann, age 57, 185 lbs., hair blond, eyes blue. Under the wallet a small pearl-handled revolver—fully loaded with six bullets—nestled in the bottom of the purse. Had Eloise left in a hurry and forgotten her purse? Or had she left it there intentionally, planning to come back for it?

I examined the dead bolt on the exit door to the left of the post office and Leroy's office. The bolt turned easily and would provide a quick exit if a warning call came from Donna. I checked my cell phone, which showed four service bars, then attacked the lock on the door to Leroy's office. It was an old Schlage lock and I was sweating under the black sweater when I finally got inside ten minutes later. I shined the flashlight on a small metal desk and three file cabinets behind it. The only windows were high and narrow, directly above the file cabinets. The plank floor squeaked as I approached the desk. One drawer in the desk was filled with old *Field and Stream* magazines; in the second drawer I found a .38 Smith & Wesson, fully loaded, and a box of ammo. None of the three metal files was locked and none of the drawers had a label to identify the contents.

The top three drawers of the first cabinet contained tax records for Leroy and Eloise going back twenty years, and a stack of loose papers that must have belonged to the fishing years in Alaska. The bottom drawer contained loose legal files marked "Homer Hausmann Will and Estate."

I closed the bottom drawer and stood up as a burst of rain hit the skylight above the desk. I hoped the night was dark enough to cover the rays from my flashlight. I checked my cell phone. The bars were down to three, which was usually enough to receive a call. The time was 9:25. I made my way quickly through the second cabinet, which was filled with odds and ends of office supplies. It was in the last cabinet that I hit pay dirt.

The top drawer contained folders with a Certificate of Formation for Santa Maria Safaris, L.L.C., a Washington limited liability company. The date of formation was over eighteen months ago. Leroy was listed as the manager, and a letter from a Seattle attorney included an admonition to be sure to file an annual report within 124 days of the date of formation. The "Purposes and Powers" of Santa Maria Safaris were "to engage in any business, trade or activity which may be conducted lawfully by a limited liability company organized under the Washington limited liability company act, RCW 25.15.et. seq., as it may be amended or revised, including without limitation the businesses of real estate investing and sales, livestock breeding, game preservation, and wildlife hunting."

There it was!

Livestock breeding, game preservation, and wildlife hunting.

I pulled my Nikon from the rucksack and photographed the pertinent pages of the formation papers. Behind the Safari files, I found several thick files of information on outfitters, guides, and hunting lodges in Washington and British Columbia, but nothing that would link the L.L.C. to Mimi's property or explain why Leroy was behind the accidents. That is, nothing until I opened the second drawer and found brown-paper packages of four-color brochures on the Santa Maria Safaris Time-Share Plan . . . *illustrated with photos of the convent property.*

I pulled a chair over to the file and began reading. Half an hour later, most of the pieces of the puzzle were falling into place. Santa Maria Safaris L.L.C., which was formed about six months before Mimi bought the convent property, was the vehicle through which Leroy intended to sell time-shares in a hunting lodge which, judging from the photos in the brochures, could only be the convent property. Each time-share included fourteen days per year at the Santa Maria Safari Lodge, three meals a day, hunting licenses, and full hunting access— depending on the season of the year—to wild turkeys, white antelope, wild pigs, and whitetail deer—on three hundred acres of rolling countryside overlooking the blue waters of the Strait of Georgia. The lodge would provide transportation from the Friday Harbor airport for prospective buyers.

I stared in disbelief at the photos of Mimi's property. The courtyard and the old vineyards. A shot of the Butterfly Meadow in full bloom. A white antelope with tall antlers grazing in tall green grass. And on the back cover, a shot of a beaming Leroy in a red-checked shirt, holding aloft one of Abigail's wild turkeys. I tucked two of the brochures in my rucksack and replaced the rest in the second drawer, opened the next drawer, riffled through the twenty or so folders, each with the name of a time-share buyer.

I was about to start photographing when I heard the sound of a vehicle outside. I stuffed the thickest of the folders in my rucksack, glanced at the cell phone. I had two missed calls and the service bars were down to two. *Merde!* Something had gone wrong, Donna had called and tried to warn me, and there hadn't been enough cell phone service to get the call through! *Merde encore!* I doused the flashlight and crawled under the desk, furious at myself for leaving the office door open. I curled into a ball on the floor under the desk, knowing that if it was Eloise who found me, she would either call the sheriff or sic Leroy and his buddies on me, and it didn't take me more than two seconds to know which I preferred. That is, if she didn't take care of me with the pearl-handled revolver first. I didn't want to even consider the outcome if it was Leroy who came crashing through the door after an evening of poker and alcohol.

Someone tried to unlock the dead bolt first, must have discovered that it wasn't locked, then turned the key in the lower lock. The door flew open and banged against the wall. It was Eloise. "Stupid idiot Leroy," she grumbled, slamming the door against the wind. For a minute I thought they both had returned, then I realized she was talking to herself. "Never remembers to put the effing dead bolt on." I heard her approach the counter, probably for the forgotten purse, a few seconds of silence, then, "Well, well, look what dummy did now. Left the office open for the whole world to find. Effing idiot."

I cursed my stupidity again as her footsteps approached the office. The steps stopped at the doorway. I prayed she couldn't hear my heart beating and couldn't see me under the desk in the darkness. Or worse yet, wouldn't turn on the office light. One of the floorboards creaked. After what seemed like an eternity, she mumbled something I couldn't make out, the office door closed, and I heard a key turn from the other side. A few seconds later, the front door shut, the dead bolt turned, a car door shut, and I heard the spinning of tires on loose gravel. Eloise was gone. I crawled out from under the desk, moved over to the door, and verified the fear that had crossed my mind when I'd heard her lock the office door. There was no access to the lock on this side.

I was trapped in Leroy's office.

Another burst of rain hit the skylight. I glanced up, considered and immediately discarded any thought of getting to the top of the room. I squinted at the file drawer I'd been checking when Eloise arrived, decided to pilfer a few more files from the back of the drawer, then zipped everything into the rucksack. Again I stared in dismay at the high, narrow windows above the file cabinets. How the hell was I going to get out of Leroy's office?

The bars on the cell phone were back up to four. I checked the call log, found Angela's home number and what looked like Donna's number. Donna answered on the first ring.

"Yeah?"

"It's Scotia. You called. What happened?"

"I saw headlights go by the house and I figured it had to be Eloise for some reason, going back to the store. I called over to Mabel's asking for her rhubarb cobbler recipe, and Mabel said Eloise drank too much wine and left early in a foul mood. Did she turn up?"

"She was here and left," I said. "Where is she now?"

"She went tearing past about five minutes ago and I saw the headlights turn into their drive. I would guess she's crashed by now. You find anything?"

"Several things. But right now I've got to break out of here."

"My God, you're locked in! You want me to come over?"

"If I can't make it out, I'll call you," I said, eyeing the tall, narrow window I was going to have to wriggle through.

Fifteen minutes later, I'd managed to climb onto the top of the file cabinets, twisted open the rusty window latch, pushed out the screen, and maneuvered my body through a window that was not more than ten inches high. Panic had set in at one point when I thought I was stuck and envisioned myself hanging head-down from the window when Leroy et al. arrived at the store the following morning. The drop to the ground was about eight feet. I landed on my shoulder in the soft mud and sat for a few minutes, moving various limbs, grateful to the mud for cushioning the fall, trying to see into the blackness.

Not wanting to press my luck by putting on the flashlight in case Eloise had called Leroy to report the open office door before she crashed, I began to feel my way along the back of the building. Halfway along, I heard a soft bleat that sounded a little like a sheep. I peered into the darkness and made out a tall fence or wall directly in front of me. I moved toward it, felt wooden boards, heard the bleating again.

All around were blackness and wind and driving rain. Praying that Leroy wouldn't be inclined to head anywhere except his own bed in such weather, I groped along the wooden fence for a handle or latch, found the latter, lifted it gently. The tall gate opened with a whiff of something that smelled like livestock, although not sheep. I peered into the enclosure, heard several more soft bleats, and then began to make out moving white shapes. I shone the flashlight briefly into startled eyes and over wet white hides. With a sinking heart, I stared at the white antelope, a confirmation that Leroy was stockpiling more than just San Juan Island wild turkeys for the Santa Maria Safaris.

15

It was nearly eleven when, sodden and tired, I got back to the hotel. The old blue slicker leaked, and the sailing boots were never meant for hiking on unpaved country roads in the dark. No head-lights followed me up the road, which meant Leroy was either still drinking and gambling up-island or tucked cozily into bed with Eloise. I picked my way across the wet courtyard to the main hotel entrance in total blackness and stepped inside. Five figures— Mimi, Graham, Joseph, Abigail, and Zelda—their faces illuminated by the blazing fire, were sitting around in the dark great room that was otherwise lit only by small oil lamps.

"What happened to the lights?" I inquired, hang-ing the slicker on a hook in the hall. "Or are we conserving energy?"

Mimi sighed. "Antonio forgot to buy diesel fuel when he was in Friday Harbor, so we can't use the generator. Anyway, Graham built this beautiful fire and found a bottle of brandy in the pantry. Come and sit, Scotia. You certainly are a fresh-air fiend to be out on a night like this." I removed the black watch cap and Mimi gave me another look. "Oh, my. Scotia, you're soaked. Were you . . . out investigating? Because of Tiffany? Because of . . . me?"

I sank into the overstuffed chair beside Graham, who handed me a small tumbler. I sniffed the brandy appreciatively. "I was out investigating because of everything," I said. "Because of Eric, because of Zoe, because of Tiffany. I may have some answers. Do you want to have my report in private?"

She shook her head. "No, I've just been saying that I'm at my wit's end. I don't know what to do." She glanced toward the windows. "Zoe's father called tonight and so did Tiffany's fiancé. Eric's out of the hospital and he wanted to talk to Tiffany. I . . . I told him she was with Natasha. I just couldn't tell him the truth. I can't even imagine Tiffany being out in this weather somewhere. It's horrible."

"Where is Eric?" I asked.

"He's at his sister's. He'll call back." She shivered. "Did you find anything that would explain what's going on?"

"It's a bit bizarre," I began, and took a sip of the brandy. "I raided the office at the General Store and found a few interesting items." I pulled the two Safari brochures out of the rucksack, handed one to Mimi, one to Graham. Graham read it, raised his eyebrows, handed it to Abigail. She scanned it quickly, slammed her glass down on the table, and stood up, glowering at the brochure.

"That jackass is going to turn his farm into a *wild-*

life preserve. With white antelope and wild pigs."
She paused, frowning, reading further. "And he's
going to sell time-shares and let people come and
shoot the animals?"

I took another sip of the brandy. "No, Abigail,
his plan is, or was, to build the Safari right *here*, on
the convent property."

"*On Mimi's property?*" Abigail's voice was so high
it squeaked.

I nodded, reaching into the rucksack and pulling
out one of the files I'd heisted. "He had this all set
up and everything was in place, except he was still
quibbling over the price when Mimi walked in and
paid the full asking price. And it wasn't just a plan.
He actually sold time-shares. At least twenty or
thirty of them at thirty thousand dollars each. And
collected the money." I opened one of the files,
scanned it, handed it to Mimi. "And now he's being
sued, since he can't produce the Safari."

We stared at each other, everyone digesting the
implications of what I'd discovered. And just how
important it had become for Leroy Hausmann that
the Rossellinis give up and leave the island.

"Sorta gives new meaning to being between a
rock and a hard place, doesn't it," Zelda observed.
On the hearth, a burning log broke in two and fell
through the grate. Red embers sprayed into the air.

"So that explains the stonemason's boat that was
set adrift," Mimi said in a soft voice. "The catalog
orders that never got delivered. And the accidents.
He killed Zoe, didn't he? And poor Tiffany? Do you
think he killed her, too?"

Silent, we all stared into our brandy glasses. From

outside, a gust of wind drove the trees against the windows.

"He's not going to give up, is he?" Mimi said. "Not until I close down the hotel and leave. And if I don't leave, there will be more accidents. My God, what am I going to do?" She buried her head in her hands. Again, none of us had an answer. Graham reached over and took her hand in his. I wondered where Piero was.

"The sheriff is sending one of the deputies tomorrow to search the island for Tiffany," Abigail announced grimly. "I'm going to make one more call to Olympia, to the Fish and Wildlife people. And if they won't do anything, there's more than one way to skin a skunk."

I swallowed the last of the brandy and stood up, cold, wet, and demoralized. What I had found in Leroy's office gave him more than enough motivation to have been behind the accidents, but I still had nothing concrete to link him to Eric or Zoe or Tiffany, and no way to help Mimi. I ached in every joint and muscle, and before I could sleep I needed to check *DragonSpray*'s lines one more time. Mimi handed me an oil lantern.

"We'll run out of water soon," she said apologetically, "but there's probably still enough hot water in the tank for a shower."

I nodded, pulled the old slicker on, and headed down to the marina.

It was after midnight when I got back to the hotel and found my way to my room. The window was closed and no big gray cat waited on the bed. I stripped down, pulled on my robe, and was about to head to the shower when I saw a piece of paper that must have been slid under my door when I was out. It was a short, handwritten note in pencil on blue-lined notebook paper. I read it with the light of the lantern.

You're probably not going to believe any of this, since you and that old cow all think you're so smart, but I saw something on Thursday night about two o'clock in the morning when I came in. It was somebody tall in blue jeans and a hat that was trying to get into Tiffany's room. They were messing with the lock, and then they opened the door. Then I went to bed. That's all I saw. I hope you find Tiffany before they kill her. And tell Mimi she should stop robbing the cradle. Rita.

My weary brain tried to assimilate Rita's grim note: Somebody tall in blue jeans had attempted and succeeded in breaking into Tiffany's room early on Thursday morning. Among the guests at the hotel, only Graham was over six feet. Antonio was not tall. I judged Leroy to be about six-four and Stuey around five-ten. I dismissed Graham, but considered it quite possible that either of the last two could have kidnaped Tiffany, particularly if Leroy had somehow learned that Tiffany's fiancé was a Venezuelan oil tycoon. I couldn't imagine where he had gotten such information, unless it had come from Rita. I recalled hearing Piero send her to the store for milk recently. Had Eloise pumped her for information on the guests? Had Leroy? A hefty ransom from the fiancé could bail Leroy out of his current financial squeeze.

Returning to my room after a brief, lukewarm shower, I heard the sounds of sobbing coming from the room next door. I tapped on the door. Danielle, wearing her white terry robe, a glass of red wine in one hand, opened it. "Is there anything I can do, Danielle?" I asked, wondering why she hadn't left on the Saturday-afternoon ferry.

She shook her head and wiped her eyes with one sleeve of the robe. "I miss Zoe so much," she said, both eyes closed. "I didn't think I would. She was such a pain. But I do. And now her father is demanding an investigation. I talked to him today. I know they're going to think I did it."

"Why would anyone think that?"

"The night before her accident, we were in the great room. Zoe said she was personally going to tell my daughters about us if I didn't. I said some awful things to her. I said if she ever said anything to any of my family, I'd kill her. I thought we were alone, but when I left, Andrea was in the hallway. I think she heard the whole thing. I don't know what to do."

"Danielle, did you push Zoe off the cliff?"

"No," she sobbed. "No. But if someone else didn't, I might have one day. That's what's so *scary*."

I regarded the distraught woman, at a loss as to how to help her. "Is there some reason you didn't leave on the ferry today?"

She nodded. "By the time the ferry got to Friday

Harbor, there would have been only one evening flight to Seattle. And that was on a small plane. With the weather so bad . . ." She shrugged helplessly.

I nodded. "It should improve by Tuesday," I assured her. "Then you'll be able to get back home."

She thanked me for trying to find out what had happened to Zoe, and I told her to be careful with the oil lantern. I closed the door softly, thinking that everything was getting more complicated by the hour. The wind was blowing the rain against the windows with malevolent force. I locked my door from the inside, wishing the hotel had a security system of some sort, although I didn't know of any lodging establishment in the San Juans that did. In fact, in a number of smaller B & Bs there were no locks on any of the rooms. But then, the other islands didn't have a Leroy Hausmann.

Through sheer exhaustion, by 1:30 I was about to fall asleep when I heard the outside door beside my room open and close. Wondering who among the few of us left was insane enough to still be wandering about in the night, I opened my door an inch or so. I peered down the dark corridor, startled to see the skirts of Serafina's drenched black cape illuminated by a large flashlight, about to turn the corner into the great room. Shaking my head in amazement, wondering what Serafina was doing in our wing, I relocked my door and returned to bed, thinking that Mimi was right: Serafina was crazy.

The wind howled ever more strongly. Curled first on my right side, then on my left, I huddled under the comforter, thinking about Nick. I was following the hands on the clock from 2:00 to 2:20 to 2:40, when I heard a loud crash in the courtyard outside my window. Seconds later a door down the hall opened. I put on my robe and slippers and peered into the passageway.

Graham stood in the corridor, clad in pajamas and a dark red wool robe. "Sounds like a tree came down," he said, holding up a lantern.

"I think so," I said, moving into the corridor. "The wind's a bit much."

"Nasty storm," he said. "I gave up sleeping around midnight, so I've been up writing. Actually, I'm worried about my sister. The situation in Venezuela is deteriorating. She thinks there's going to be another attempt at a coup and this time it might succeed."

"So there would be one less totalitarian regime in Latin America. Wouldn't that be a good thing?" I asked, slightly hysterical at the thought of discussing foreign politics in the dark in the middle of a raging storm.

Graham shook his head. "The current regime is authoritarian and oppressive, but the president is just a two-bit tropical despot and his ham-handed attempts at autocracy are a long way from the terror and mass-scale violence that permeates anything you could halfway call totalitarian."

There was another crash outside, not as loud as the previous one. I flinched and pulled my robe tighter.

"There goes another tree," Graham said. "Mimi's going to have a mess to clean up."

I nodded, thinking that she had a far bigger mess on her hands than just fallen trees.

"I'm worried about her," Graham said. "What do you think is going on? You think that Leroy guy is behind all the incidents? Eric and Zoe's accidents? And now Tiffany?"

"It's possible," I said, thinking of Rita's note. "It's also possible that Eric and Zoe really did have accidents and that Tiffany decided to take French leave. Maybe she hired somebody to pick her up in a boat."

"That's very optimistic of you, Scotia." Graham yawned. "There's something I've been meaning to mention. The first night we were here, Tuesday night after dinner, Andrea and I were standing outside in the courtyard getting some fresh air. Tiffany came outside, walked across the courtyard toward the far door, and Eric, the photographer fellow, came out of the great room and followed her. I don't think they saw us. They appeared to know each other quite well, if you understand my meaning. They embraced for a long time, then went inside together. The light came on in one of the rooms facing the courtyard. I saw them together before she pulled the drapes." He yawned again. "Isn't she supposed to be engaged or something?"

"Her fiancé's name is Roberto Velásquez del Pino," I said, wondering if Zelda had gotten the background check on Roberto. "A Venezuelan, actually."

Graham raised his eyebrows. "Velásquez is almost as common in Latin America as Smith is here, but one of the oil-strike leaders who started the last coup was a guy by the name of Velásquez del Pino. Old Caracas family that hated the president. He fled the country when the coup didn't succeed." He chuckled. "Good thing Roberto wasn't lurking around on Tuesday night. It's virtually a tradition for a Venezuelan of del Pino's stature to have a mistress, but just let the little woman start playing around and she's toast."

"She said he's got a lot of money. Oil money."

Graham nodded. "If it's the same guy, Tiffany is playing in the big leagues."

I felt goose bumps come up on my arms. Cuckolding a Latin-American oil tycoon was definitely playing in the big leagues.

16

I don't know that I ever really slept for the rest of that predawn Sunday morning. There were brief, thin dreams of cold rain and long grass and the mournful, eerie notes of Graham's Japanese flute threaded with fragments of my conversation with Melissa over my not going to the Seychelles with Simon all those years ago. And underlying all of it, the frustration of not having concrete evidence to link Leroy Hausmann with the incidents that were driving Mimi off the island.

Around 7:30 I heard the big door beside my room open. A gust of wind rushed under my door, followed by impatient knocking. I pulled the drapes open and grabbed a robe. It was Zelda, freckles standing out on her pale face, red hair hanging in a tangled mop. She was wrapped in an old tan trenchcoat, a pair of red boots on her feet.

"Sorry to wake you so early, boss. Everything's going from bad to worse."

"If that's possible," I said, glancing out the window. The rain had stopped and the sky was full of low, dark, fast-moving clouds.

"We haven't seen Serafina since yesterday afternoon and Piero's frantic. He heard about Leroy's plan for the convent and he's convinced that Leroy kidnaped his aunt to get leverage over Mimi, since he hasn't been able to scare her off the island. He says it happens all the time in Italy."

"Serafina came in really late last night," I said, frowning, thinking about the hooded black figure that had been scurrying about the hotel for the past few days, remembering with a jolt *exactly* where I'd seen her black cloak hanging once before. "She must have left early this morning. You might find her at Gus's place."

"Gus's? What's she doing at Gus's? Anyway, the other reason I came over is that I forgot to give you the background report on Tiffany's fiancé last night." She handed me a printed sheet with the DataTech logo. The info was brief. Roberto Velásquez del Pino had been born in Caracas forty-three years ago, had been married to and divorced from Mariana Castellano de León. He had a law degree from the Univerisad de Caracas and had held several executive-level positions with Petróleos de Venezuela, S.A. The report included translations of newspaper articles that had appeared in *Ultimas Noticias* and *Meridiano* in the six months before the attempted coup, all indicating that del Pino had been at the forefront of the striking executives trying to oust the president. He had no police record in the U.S. One last newspaper article was attached, a short column from the Nuptials section of the *San Diego Tribune*. It described the sumptuous celebration at the home of Roberto del Pino of La Jolla, announcing his engagement to Ms. Tiffany Marr of San Francisco.

"Anything you didn't already know, boss?"

I shook my head, noticing for the first time the cell phone she was holding. "You get a new cell phone?"

"It's Andrea's. She left it in the bathroom. She's got text messaging. There are three messages from a Roberto, but they're in Spanish."

"Roberto as in *Tiffany's* Roberto?"

"Has to be. I checked the hotel's incoming phone log. There were seven messages from a La Jolla number, which are on the carbon copy in the hotel message book. The phone number's the same as on the text messages." She handed me the tiny silver cell phone and indicated a button below the backlit green screen. "Press this button and you can scroll through them."

I recalled the times I'd seen Andrea in the phone booth outside the dining room, and once standing on the hillside below the vineyard with her cell phone. I read the first message, which had come in on Tuesday morning. *Pantera mia—Llamame cuando llegas. Roberto*

"What does it say?" Zelda asked.

"My panther. Call me when you arrive."

"My *panther*? What's that? A love name?"

"I don't know. Maybe."

"What about the other two messages?"

The second one was sent on Thursday. I read the

message and translated. *"Pantera: que paso con la periodista? La hiciste?* What happened with the journalist? Did you do her?"

"The journalist?"

"Probably Zoe."

"He's asking if Andrea *murdered* her?"

I shrugged, scrolling to the third message. "Could be."

Por que no respondes a mis llamadas? Por que dejaste al fotografo escapar? Donde esta la puta?

I read it twice and translated for Zelda. "Why haven't you responded to my calls? Why did you let the photographer escape? Where is the whore?"

"Why hasn't she returned his *calls*?" Zelda asked. "Guess she hasn't clued him about the cell phone service on Santa Maria. What's the bit about letting the photographer escape? And the *whore*?"

The pieces were beginning to fall into place faster than I could process them. *Tiffany's creative director who had a fatal skiing accident in Switzerland. Graham and Andrea seeing Eric and Tiffany together the first night of the retreat.*

"In the traditional Hispanic concept of honor," I explained, "once a wife or fiancée is unfaithful to her husband, she's no better than a prostitute. Gives her husband the right to kill her."

Zelda shivered. "Sounds like sixteenth-century opera."

"It actually comes from the four-hundred-year Moorish occupation of Spain. Anyway, my guess is that Roberto found out that Tiffany had a fling with Eric in California—" I began.

"You mean when she did the modeling assignment with him?

"Yes," I said, thinking of the nude photo I'd found in Tiffany's suitcase.

"And he sent Andrea to spy on them? Or to kill them? My God!"

I nodded again, remembering Graham's comments about the sexual double standard of Latin men and that Tiffany was playing in the big leagues. "I also think Eric's accident was just that. An accident. He ignored the sign on the old stairway, slipped and fell to the bottom, and was medevaced off the island before Andrea could get to him. It probably saved his life."

"But why Andrea? Who is she? Roberto's mistress? His secretary? A contract killer?"

"Any or all of the above," I said slowly, staring at the last text message. "And probably not a social worker. At least not the kind we know."

"But why Zoe? What did *she* have to do with Tiffany and Eric?"

"I'm not sure about Zoe, yet. She must have gotten in the way." I thought about Rita seeing someone trying to unlock Tiffany's room as I scrolled rapidly through the three messages again, bits and pieces of the last five days flooding my mind.

Serafina's long black cloak that had been thrown over the chair at Gus's place.

The food and towels missing from the hotel.

The undersheriff's frustrated complaint when I'd called to report Tiffany missing: "I'm sitting here staring at a box of audio cassettes that just came in from some kook on Santa Maria who says he thinks a bunch of South Americans are planning an assassination!"

The brief encounter I'd witnessed between Gus and Tiffany in the courtyard the night before she disappeared.

The state-of-the-art audio equipment I'd glimpsed at Gus's, including a scanner that could be used to monitor cell phone conversations.

Andrea raising an arm to comb back her hair, a tiny black panther tattooed on the inside of her elbow.

Pantera mia!

And finally, the partially remembered fragment of conversation I'd overheard between Zoe and Danielle: " . . . *story I was working on last year . . . gangs . . . tattoo is identical.*"

"I don't know how Andrea and Roberto are related, but I think I know where Tiffany is. And I've got to get to her before Andrea finds her!"

PART 3

Punishment is justice for the unjust.
—St. Augustine

17

While I grabbed a pair of blue jeans from my suitcase and put them on, I told Zelda briefly what I'd deduced. "I'm going up to the pay phone and make a couple of quick calls, then I'm going over to Gus's. See if you can locate Andrea and let me know where she is."

I grabbed the Beretta from the rucksack, raced down the corridor, across the great room, and up the stairs. The phone booth was empty. I closed the folding glass door and dialed the San Juan County Sheriff's department. Neither Jeffrey Fountain nor Angela Petersen was in. I left a message on Jeff's voice mail telling him the conclusions I'd come to about Andrea and where I thought Tiffany was or had been. I asked for backup. Hoping that cell coverage would be better on the other side of the hill, I left my cell phone number and was heading for the stairway when Mimi emerged from her office.

"Scotia, this must fax have come in for you before we lost power yesterday."

The fax was on KKSB Santa Barbara letterhead and contained a draft of the news report Zoe had been working on when she was suspended. I read it quickly. It confirmed part of my theory about Andrea, but with an unexpected twist.

> Las Panteras: Female Assassins for the 21st Century?
> Gangs in Los Angeles are not news, but a litter of Columbian and Venezuelan prostitutes turned killers for hire who call themselves Las Panteras (The Panthers) is something else entirely. . . .

The summary explained that Las Panteras had been the brainchild of a reformed Caracas prostitute who worked with martial-arts and weapons experts to train a select group of her sisters from the streets to become high-priced assassins back in the nineties. Her theory was that a good-looking woman posing as a call girl could get much closer to her target—usually a man—than a male assassin. After initial success in Latin America, she began to send her protégées on assignments to the northern hemisphere—Los Angeles, Chicago, New York—where they would romance their targets, strike, and disappear. With the expansion of the drug scene in the U.S., and increasing turf wars between Colombian, Mexican, and Asian drug lords, her client list had grown.

Based on an interview with an L.A.P.D. detective who had arrested a Colombian woman before the woman was found dead in her cell with a cyanide capsule between her back molars, Zoe's article hypothesized that each of the Panteras had a small black panther tattoo somewhere on her body.

Footsteps pounded up the stairs. It was Zelda. "Andrea's gone," she said breathlessly. "Antonio saw her leave the hotel half an hour ago. She wanted to take the van, but he told her Black Raven Road was flooded. She headed over the hill on foot."

"Call Gus's house," I said, racing past her and checking the pocket of my foul-weather jacket for the Beretta. "Tell him I'm on my way, and not to let anyone else in except the sheriff."

Fallen madrona trees littered the courtyard. The path behind the hotel that led up to the Butterfly Meadow was muddy and slippery. In the steepest places water gushed downhill in torrents.

Someone in a pair of boots larger than mine had recently climbed the steep trail. Twice I slipped in the mud and grabbed at a tree for support. Gusts well over thirty knots howled over the cliff and across the meadow. The path around the bushes of Nootka roses was underwater. Passing the overlook where Zoe had fallen to her death, I was facing directly into the wind. I tucked my chin inside my jacket and stayed well away from the edge of the bluff. Halfway down the hill on the other side I paused in a grove of madrona trees. A plume of smoke from Gus's chimney blew across the valley. The big, dark horse he'd called Sebastian was in the corral, munching his morning ration of hay. I didn't see the golden retriever. As I considered my options, my cell phone rang. It was Jeffrey Fountain.

"It all fits, Scotia," he said. "I listened to the audio tapes last night with Maria, my sister-in-law. She translated them for me and I figured out it wasn't just some kook. Gus Lindstrom, the guy who used to be the gardener at the convent, recorded them. When you called and told me about the missing woman's fiancé being Latin and jealous, it kinda all came together."

"Exactly what's on the tapes, Jeff?"

"Four conversations between a man and a woman in Spanish. One of the conversations cuts in and out. Sounds like the photographer was the woman's first target. When he fell down the stairs and got himself transported off-island, they went after the TV woman. And the missing model, Tiffany Marr, she was next. I tried to call Gus, but he's not answering the phone. Where are you now? Do you know if Tiffany is still OK?"

"I'm looking at Gus's place right now. I don't know the answer to the second question. Will you be able to get over here in this storm?"

"Wind's supposed to lay down pretty soon. We'll do our best. I don't think we can set the helicopter down there near Gus's place. Too rough and hilly. I do recall that there's a flat meadow on the west side of the island, right above where the TV woman fell."

"Set it down there. It's only half a mile or so from Gus's."

I told him about Zoe's article, and that Andrea might be a hired killer.

"If she is, she'll probably be armed to the teeth. Don't do anything before we get there."

"If I wait, there may not be anyone to rescue. Call me when you set down in the meadow."

I began to move from tree to tree down the rocky hillside, skirting the clearing until I was at the back of the stable on the lower level, below a hay loft and Gus's living quarters, all the time considering the implications of taking on a trained assassin. Twice I thought I heard shouts. As I opened the gate to the small corral, my cell phone rang again. It was Zelda. Gus didn't answer his phone, she reported. She didn't think it wise to leave a recorded message.

Eyeing Sebastian, who continued munching his hay while watching me walk to the stable door, Beretta in hand, I stepped inside where the stable smelled of horse manure and grain and hay and old dust. Again I heard a shout, and something heavy fell to the floor of the room above me. I moved quickly across the horse stall, avoiding the piles of fresh manure, reached over the top of the stall gate, and let myself out into a narrow aisle that ended at a door.

Another shout came from above; this time Gus's voice, followed by a dog's whimper. The door at the end of the aisle opened into a narrow corridor with two doors and a narrow, circular wooden stairway that led to the top floor. Whatever was going on in the place, it all seemed to be happening on the upper level. Expecting to hear a shot at any moment, I quickly checked out the two lower rooms, both of which were bedrooms. The one with the unmade bed and dirty overalls draped over a ladder-back wooden chair clearly belonged to Gus. The other had a handmade quilt on the bed, also unmade, a lavender shirt I'd seen Tiffany wear earlier in the week, her gray suede walking shoes, and a pair of faded blue jeans. A white towel with the Dei Fiori monogram hung from a hook on the wall.

Once more something dropped or was thrown on the floor upstairs. Heart pounding, I closed the bedroom door and regarded the wooden stairway, considered and rejected the idea of trying to storm the upper level from there.

I quickly retraced my steps back through Sebastian's corral and let myself out the gate beside the house. Hugging the rough stone, I crawled up the steep, muddy hillside until my head was almost level with one of the windows in the main living quarters. The window was open two or three inches and I heard Andrea's frenzied voice.

". . . mine! Mine long before he saw you, you filthy pig. I told him not to fuck with white-skinned whores."

I stood on tiptoe, inched up to the window, and took in the tragedy unfolding inside. Andrea's long hair was loose around her head. Her face looked almost feral. Her back was to the main door and she was holding Tiffany and Gus and Serafina at bay with a small gun. All three were seated around a wooden table and had their hands in the air. Three coffee mugs, the remains of the banana bread and a platter of what looked like scrambled eggs were on the table. The Golden cowered on the floor near the fireplace. I remembered the shout and the dog's whimper while I was below and wondered if Andrea had harmed the dog. Tiffany, wearing a grotty faded maroon bathrobe that probably belonged to Gus, was barefoot. A glass vase lay shattered on the floor near her left foot. Serafina, clad in her voluminous black cape, was seated between Tiffany and Gus, her face screwed up in a scowl. Andrea held the small gun with both hands at shoulder level, aiming it first toward Gus, then back toward Tiffany. Her anger made her English hard to understand and for a few seconds I thought she was speaking Spanish. As I listened, I understood for the first time that she had more than one motive for going after Tiffany.

"I am with him for five years," she hissed. "I kill for him, I give him a son. Then he meets you and I have to leave his house."

"He was only divorced three years ago," Tiffany countered, reaching down to pull the front of the old bathrobe together. Her voice was steady, her face pale.

"*Manos arriba!*" Andrea screamed, waving the gun. Tiffany's eyes closed for a long second, then she raised her arm again as Andrea continued her tirade.

"*Puta mentirosa! Robert es mío!* He is Carlito's father. We sleep together, even when he is engaged to you. I will go back to Caracas with him."

Tiffany shrugged, but her face went paler. "Andrea, he's all yours, you can have him. I'm sorry, I didn't know—"

"It is too *late, puta fea*. Of course I will have him. And you and your lover will burn in hell!"

I moved back from the window, my heart beating so hard I could scarcely hear. I scanned the sky for a helicopter, saw nothing but dark clouds, mentally replayed what I'd glimpsed through the window and considered my options.

The door was around the corner to my left. There was nothing to stand on and it would be very difficult to get off an accurate shot through the window above my head. If I missed, the consequences were not nice to contemplate. As I scanned the empty sky one more time, I knew the one and only chance I would have to save any of the people inside was to burst through the door behind Andrea so fast and with enough force to momentarily confuse her, then pray that the three would have the sense to get out of her line of sight. And pray also that at least one of the three would take some defensive action until I could disable or disarm her.

A stone moved under my foot, I grabbed at the side of the house for balance. The Golden raised his head, looked toward the window and barked twice. I had to go in now or it would be too late. I ducked my head, checked the safety on the Beretta, and moved swiftly under the window and around the corner toward the front door. The latch was black wrought iron, the kind you open by pressing down with your thumb. I would have only one chance. Praying that Andrea still had her back to the door, I took a deep breath, pressed down on the latch with my left hand and crashed into the room with every ounce of strength I possessed. She outweighed me by at least twenty pounds, but the force of the sudden intrusion pushed her violently into the room. She stumbled, but did not drop the gun. I darted to one side of the room as Andrea fell heavily to the floor, recovered, and came up on one knee, shrieking and shooting. I zigzagged, felt one bullet whistle over my shoulder, heard two more hit the wall to my right, whirled, raised the Beretta, and aimed for Andrea's right hand. I squeezed the trigger a nanosecond after Serafina brought a large clay pot down on Andrea's head with the force of someone twice her size.

"*Asassina!*" Serafina shrieked as the bullet from the Beretta hit the hearth and Andrea collapsed in a heap, her gun clattering to the floor. The Golden gave a long howl and leaped for Gus's side. For several seconds, the four of us stared at the beautiful woman with tawny skin who had turned so deadly, then I sprang across the room and checked Andrea's carotid artery. She was alive and breathing. A narrow stream of blood was beginning to trickle out of her hair and down across her forehead. Using a large roll of gray duct tape, we tied Andrea's hands and feet, removed a small, thin, deadly looking dagger from a thigh holster, found a second small pistol in a bra holster, and managed to call the undersheriff as he was circling over the Butterfly Meadow.

It was ten thirty by the time our band had climbed up the hill and arrived back at the meadow, a now-conscious and livid Andrea tied across Sebastian's broad back, duct tape wrapped across her mouth. Gus led Sebastian and I followed the huge hooves of the big black horse, replaying the morning's events, reflecting that Andrea was a lousy assassin. The only thing that had saved Tiffany from death the minute Andrea arrived at Gus's place—and probably Gus and Serafina as well—was Andrea's emotional involvement with Roberto. I was convinced that her original assignment was simply to attend the retreat and to kill Eric—as the creative director had been eliminated in Switzerland.

Sometime during the week, probably after glimpsing the tiny panther tattoo, Zoe had guessed that Andrea was one of the Panteras she was investigating. And—in Zoe's inimitable fashion—perhaps had confronted her. Following Zoe's murder, whether at Roberto's request or on her own, Andrea had made Tiffany her next target. After listening to the tapes Gus gave her, Tiffany had fled to the stone cottage, perhaps hours or minutes before Andrea had attempted to enter her room on Thursday night. And, ultimately, Andrea had to tell Tiffany how much she hated her, had to make sure Tiffany died knowing that she, Andrea, had a prior and future claim on Roberto. Eric had fortuitously escaped, but if Andrea's plans had not gone awry, I had no doubt that after killing Tiffany, her next task would have been to track him down.

The San Juan County Sheriff's helicopter was waiting in the meadow, Jeffrey and Angela and another deputy I didn't know pacing around the whirlybird. We handed Andrea over, watched them cuff her and carry her aboard, her face writhing in fury. "Be very careful with this one," I cautioned Angela. "If she's who we think she is, she's not used to failing."

Angela nodded. "This lady is going to bypass Friday Harbor. The sheriff of Island County has a cell all ready for her." She closed the door of the helicopter and the big bird darted away.

"Aren't you going with them?" I asked Angela, watching Gus give Tiffany a long hug and then turn Sebastian around to head home. Frowning, Tiffany stared after the man and the big dark horse for a minute, glanced in the other direction across the meadow to where Serafina's dark, hooded figure was disappearing over the hill back toward the hotel, and began to cry.

I moved closer to her and touched her arm. "It's all over, Tiffany," I said. "Andrea is going to jail. The sheriff has the tapes of her conversations with Roberto. They'll both be under arrest for conspiracy."

She shook her head. "No," she said, her voice thick with tears. "It will never be over. They'll never arrest Roberto. You don't know him. Andrea didn't get to Eric, but Roberto will send someone else. Neither of us will ever be safe." She pulled away from my hand and stumbled across the meadow behind Serafina.

I watched her retreating body, buffeted by the strong wind, then glanced back at Angela, wondering again why she hadn't left on the helicopter with the prisoner.

"While we were on the way over," Angela explained, "we got a report of another accident over here. A guy by the name of Leroy Hausmann got trampled to death by a herd of wild antelope. His neighbor, name of Mulvaney, was gored when he tried to save Hausmann. The woman who called in was ranting about two animal-rights terrorists in ski masks who let the antelope out of the corral and then turned a bunch of wild turkeys loose. I thought there might be an extra vehicle at the hotel I could use to investigate."

I stared at her, dumfounded. Abigail had done it again. And Zelda had probably aided and abetted her.

Death is not amusing, but considering Leroy's history with people and animals—the teenager who was raped, the dogs viciously beaten in Colorado, the theft of the wild turkeys from San Juan Island, the arrogant marketing of Mimi's property as a game preserve—I could not stop the hysterical wave of laughter that bubbled up in my throat. "Oh, my God," I said breathlessly. "Oh, my God. Divine justice."

"What are you talking about, Scotia? Are you okay?"

I nodded, trying to control my laughter, realizing that while Angela was my best friend, she was also a law enforcement officer. "Never mind, it's been a hard week. Come on. Let's get back to the hotel."

She gave me a strange look and we followed the others back down the hill. It was a little after noon when we got back to the Dei Fiori. The latest storm had passed over and the courtyard was bathed in spring sunshine. The fallen trees had been cut up into firewood. Tiffany, silent and pale, headed for her room. Troubled, I watched her disappear into the west wing, knowing as she did that having Andrea in custody was no guarantee of Tiffany's safety from Roberto's long reach. Andrea would be allowed one phone call from jail and then Roberto would know his pantera had failed in her mission. He would also know he could be implicated. With all of his millions, he would have at least one very competent attorney who would keep both of them out of jail, at least until a trial was scheduled. How was I going to protect Tiffany? And finally, was there any real basis to Zoe's story on *Las Panteras*? Was Andrea a member of some international group of female assassins?

Serafina, her long black cape floating behind her, disappeared in the opposite direction in search of Piero. Zelda and Jean Pierre were having a private session with Joseph on *yoga nidra*. John Jordan had brought over some diesel fuel, so power and light, if not serenity, had been restored. Graham and Mimi were in the library watching CNN. Zelda had shared my conclusions regarding Andrea and why she was at the retreat. Mimi leaped to her feet when we came in, her face pale. "You got there in time?" she asked with a tremor in her voice.

I nodded, introduced Angela, and provided a brief and somewhat sanitized account of the near-fatal events that had transpired in Gus's stable.

Mimi glanced at Angela and I explained why Deputy Petersen needed to borrow the hotel van.

"*Leroy was trampled?*" she repeated, one hand covering her mouth. Her eyes met mine and I nodded. "Oh, my God," she said. "Angela, of course you can borrow the van." With one last incredulous glance over her shoulder, she departed with Angela to get the keys and I collapsed into a chair.

"What's happening in the world?" I inquired wearily, focusing on a smart-looking Hispanic woman standing in front of a bombed-out building. ". . . another night of mass demonstrations and widespread looting. The president insists that the ten thousand signatures on the referendum requiring his removal are bogus, and vows he will continue in the presidency. This is Cristina Caviedes, signing off in Caracas."

I glanced at Graham. "Is this what you were expecting?"

He nodded. "I thought it might be over by now, but this guy's tough. I don't want to think about what will happen if he can keep the military behind him. I couldn't get through to my sister."

I thought about Roberto del Pino and Tiffany's fear that he would come after her and Eric. And flashed on Andrea's statement that she was going to return to Venezuela with Roberto. "Graham, you mentioned a group of Venezuelan exiles in Southern California. Do you think they'll try to return home?"

"Too early to say," he said.

At lunch, seated between Zelda and Jean Pierre, I learned that Antonio's girlfriend was arriving on the Tuesday ferry to fill Rita's place. The same ferry Serefina and Piero would be departing on. Jean Pierre was going to take over in the kitchen until a new chief could be recruited. And happily for Mimi,

Abigail had persuaded the Washington chapter of National Wildlife Photographers to hold a week-long meeting in June at the Dei Fiori. Neither Serefina nor Tiffany was in the dining room.

Graham, Abigail, and Danielle sat silently at the far end of the table, all seemingly lost in their own thoughts. Abigail looked up, her eyes met mine, and I thought I caught a brief smirk before she returned to her baby spinach salad with ricotta and glazed walnuts. I watched her for a minute, wondering where she and my intrepid assistant had disposed of the ski masks.

Danielle was still lingering over a coffee gelato as the others began to leave. I took my own dish of dessert and moved to a chair across from her. She looked up with a tentative smile.

"Zelda said you believe Andrea killed Zoe," she said. "That it has something to do with the story she was working on."

I told her about the draft of the news feature Zoe's supervisor had faxed to me. "Apparently, two of the women who had been caught had a black panther tattoo. When I got a glimpse of the tattoo on Andrea's wrist—" I paused as Serafina burst suddenly into the dining room, nodded curtly to us, and marched through the swinging door into the kitchen.

". . . you put two and two together," Danielle said.

"More or less."

We both turned toward the kitchen, where Serafina's voice was raised in loud and indignant Italian.

I listened, managed to understand the gist of the dressing-down Piero was getting, and couldn't repress a smile. Danielle looked at me questioningly. "Serafina is not happy with her nephew's behavior," I explained. "She's furious that he couldn't keep his hands off Rita and now she's got to leave. Apparently, he's just like his papa."

"Had his tush in a buttercup and didn't know it," she observed, scraping the last of the gelato out of the dish. "I vaguely recall Zoe saying something about a tattoo." She shook her head. "She must have decided to confront her. Zoe was one terrific investigative reporter, but never knew when to stop. Subtlety and discretion were not her high points."

I shared what I had deduced about Andrea being sent to kill Eric and that Zoe simply got in her way.

She sighed and gazed through the window for a long minute, biting her bottom lip. "Bizarre. Wrong place, wrong time. If we'd gone anywhere else . . ."

"I'm very sorry about what happened, Danielle." After a minute, I asked, "Are you going back to Santa Barbara?"

"I am. And I'm *really* going back home. Marty has a new girlfriend. He's going to move in with her and I'll have the house back. My daughters are spending the summer with me."

We stood up and listened to the voices in the kitchen, which were rising again.

"Something like, 'This is as good as it gets and you screwed it up'?" Danielle asked with a smile and a glance at the kitchen door.

"Pretty close," I said, and followed her into the hallway.

Angela returned the hotel minivan at 2:15 after determining that Stuart Mulvaney's wounds were superficial and would not require hospitalization. The EMS unit had flown in and removed Leroy's remains in a body bag. Angela reported that Eloise had been rather sanguine about Leroy's violent end, and her vow to track down the "terrorists" had been less than convincing.

In view of Zoe's death and Andrea's arrest, the sheriff had instructed Angela to take statements from all the hotel staff and guests regarding the week's events. She finished about six and I walked her down to the dock to meet the sheriff's boat. They were tying up as we came down the ramp.

"It was Cathy, wasn't it, that I saw with Nick last night?" she said, giving me a hug. "I'm really sorry. Have you heard from him?"

I stepped back and stared at her. "What are you talking about, Angela?"

"You didn't get my message last night?"

"What message?" Then I remembered: Angela's was the second call that I hadn't answered because of no cell service during my B & E at the Santa Maria General Store. After what I'd found in Leroy's files, I'd forgotten to listen to the message later. I shook my head.

"There was a drunk-and-disorderly call at the Roche Harbor bar last night just before I got off duty," she said. "Nick was there with a tall, nicely dressed couple—I think it was his partner and the guy's wife you introduced me to last year. A small blonde who looked like she'd had a lot of bubbly was hanging on Nick's arm. I hated to be the one to tell you, but . . ."

I continued staring at her, speechless. Cathy and Nick's partner's wife were best friends. The small blonde was Cathy. Nick had brought Cathy to the island, to his house on Crow's Nest Drive, last night. He had forgotten about our getaway to Victoria. And if I called him at that moment I knew exactly what he would say. *Cathy got very depressed after the wedding, Scotty. She had too much champagne and couldn't stop crying. She didn't have anywhere to go. Nicole and Larry were staying in my condo, so I thought it would be good for her to come up to the island for the night. It doesn't mean anything, Scotty. Blah, blah, blah. Yada, yada, yada.*

At the end of the dock, the deputy waved impatiently. "Hey, Angela, let's go!"

She touched my arm. "Are you going to be okay, Scotia?"

I nodded. My heart should have been breaking, but it wasn't. I should have been crying, but instead I smiled, suddenly very much okay. And like Tiffany, a free woman. "Go, Angela. I'm just fine. I've got a hot date at the Empress Hotel."

I waved as the boat powered away, then raced up the ramp and back to the hotel, impatient to get to Mimi's computer and send my acceptance to Falcon. And to try to get answers to the two remaining questions in the Dei Fiori case.

18

I was awakened on Tuesday morning, a little before seven thirty, by the caress of a furry paw on my face. It wasn't Mao, but rather Calico who'd found her way though the aft porthole I always leave open for her when I'm at the dock. I reached one hand from underneath the comforter and stroked her head. Her purring was at least two bars louder than usual; she was as glad to see me as I was glad to be back. And today I was going to see Falcon.

Running mostly on adrenaline, I'd arrived at the dock in Friday Harbor on Monday afternoon after a three-hour reach across Boundary Pass and down San Juan Channel in a steady, brisk twelve-knot breeze under blue skies. Calico stopped kneading my chest and curled up next to my right leg as the phone rang. It was Graham.

"Scotia, if you're near a television, you might want to put on CNN."

"Hold on." I scrambled out of bed, moved Cailco

up to my pillow, and wrapped the comforter around me. After a shower last night, I hadn't been able to find my pj's and had crawled into bed in my bare skin. I found the TV remote on the shelf above the table in the main salon and clicked up the news channel.

". . . again we are confirming that the Aerolíneas Venezolanas B-727 that took off from Los Angeles International Airport at 11:24 last night en route to Caracas, Venezuela, blew up over the Pacific Ocean two hundred miles from its destination. Twenty-two Venezuelan nationals were on board. At midnight last night in Caracas, after nearly seventy-two hours of street demonstrations and around-the-clock looting, the president has resigned. For an update, we go now to Cristina Caviedes in Caracas."

I pressed the mute button and turned back to the phone.

"You think he was on board, Graham?"

"Del Pino? I'd bet on it," he said. "That little community of exiles has been orchestrating the referendum and uprising for months. Somebody leaked something and got a bomb on board. Anything else is just too coincidental."

I had to know. For my own peace of mind and for Tiffany's. "Graham, I'm going to make a call. Where are you now?"

"In Mimi's office. Call me if you find out anything."

I scrambled in my rucksack for my notebook and dialed the phone number Zelda had identified a Roberto's. The phone was answered by a woman with a tremulous voice. "*Aló?*"

In my best Spanish-language impersonation I asked for Señor Velásquez del Pino. There was a gasp, then dead air, then a tearful anguished response. *"No está. Estaba en el avión. Está . . . muerto."*
He is not here. He was on the airplane. He is dead.

I expressed a condolence—one I had heard many times when my second husband, who was Mexican American, had been killed—and broke the connection. I called the hotel back and told Graham what I had learned. "Is Tiffany still around?" I asked. "I'd like to talk to her."

"Yeah, she's downstairs waiting for the van to go to the ferry. She looks like she's been crying all night. I'll get her."

Tiffany came to the phone and I told her what I had just learned.

There were a couple seconds of dead air, then a gasp. "Oh, my God, Scotia, thank you so much. He's dead. I'm . . . I'm a free woman again! I have to call Eric."

I wished her well, found a can of cat food for Calico, and was about to check out my wardrobe for something appropriate for a dinner date with a handsome agent from MI6 when the phone rang. It was Angela.

"Ready for the next episode from *la pantera*?"

"Sure. What's happening? Any word from Oak Harbor?"

"I just got a call from the sheriff. Andrea made her one call to what's his name, Roberto somebody?

"Velásquez del Pino."

"Yeah, del Pino. Apparently he promised to have her out of jail by yesterday afternoon. When that didn't happen, the fierce *pantera* had a tantrum and said she was ready to tell everything. Says del Pino sent her to Santa Maria to kill the photographer, but she was foiled when he fell down the stairs and was medevaced off the island. She wasn't sure, but thinks del Pino sent somebody to try to get to him at Harborview."

"What about Zoe?"

"The Santa Barbara TV woman? Apparently Zoe saw Andrea's panther tattoo and tried to interview her. When Andrea refused, Zoe said she was going to put her into the story anyway and Andrea stabbed her with that little dagger you found before she dumped her over the cliff. The M.E. never found the knife wound."

"What about Tiffany? Was murdering her part of Andrea's assignment?"

"Apparently Andrea deviated a bit on that one when her jealousy got the best of her. She says Tiffany deserved to die. She's scheduled for arraignment this afternoon. The court will appoint her an attorney if del Pino's lawyer doesn't show."

"I don't think that's going to happen," I said. I explained what had happened to the Venezuelan airliner.

"The saga continues, doesn't it? Hold on a minute, Scotia, I've got another call."

I waited, glancing out over the choppy blue waves of the harbor. The green-and-white inter-island *Hiyu* was pulling slowly into the ferry dock. The same ferry that had taken the Dei Fiori guests to Santa Maria just seven days ago.

"I've got to run, Scotia. A vandalism report out

at Mineral Point. Before I go, what's that you were saying about a hot date at the Empress? Is all forgiven with Nick?"

"Nick's history. And I'll tell you about the Empress when I get back."

"At first we thought it was just a rumor. Or what's referred to on the Internet as an urban legend." Michael Farraday swirled the crimson liquid and slowly emptied the crystal goblet. As charming and cosmopolitan as my dinner companion was, I would have expected him to order French wine. Instead, we were enjoying a pricey Classico Chianti. I watched his long fingers as he held the delicate stemware, noticed the curly dark hairs on the tops of his fingers, glanced involuntarily toward his chest.

"Not that there haven't been female assassins around the world," he continued. "And at various times in history. They can be quite effective for some of the very reasons that your unfortunate TV woman enumerated." He put the wine goblet back on the snowy tablecloth. He smiled and his eyes held mine. "I'm delighted you accepted my invitation, Scotia. I didn't think you would."

The sommelier, who'd been hovering at a discreet distance, moved closer. "May I refill your glasses, monsieur?"

Farraday glanced at me and I nodded, noting that his eyes were darker brown than I'd remembered. They also had depths of intelligence and humor I'd only suspected. "Just the lad," he said. The waiter removed our salad plates and served coq au vin accompanied by an artful presentation of garlic mashed potatoes. I studied Farraday's face with its high cheekbones and Roman nose.

"Italian on my mother's side," he said, insisting on providing me with a brief family tree—what he termed a "proper introduction"—over the tiny puff pastries with which we'd begun the meal in the Empress Room. "And Scottish on my father's. Highland Scot. Which was, coincidentally, what my grandmother Jessica had claimed to be. I hadn't asked yet if Farraday was his real name. Nor had I ever been clear as to whether he worked for MI5 or MI6.

When he'd picked me up the airport in Friday Harbor at three o'clock, I'd noticed that his face looked thinner than the year before. He was leaning against the fuselage of a little red and white Cessna 210 when I came through the metal gate at the end of the private section of the airfield, and gave me a very British, "Hullo, madame investigator, glad you could make it." When I extended my hand, he took it and kissed the tips of my fingers, then helped me into the right side of the plane. When we landed at the Victoria airport twenty minutes later, a taxi was waiting to deliver us to the Empress.

"To continue," he said, picking up an ornate silver knife and fork and contemplating the presentation of the coq au vin, "after I got your e-mail, I put in a request to our research department. This morning I received confirmation that Interpol has been tracking a series of assassinations which were assumed to have been carried out by a female. The *modus operandus* was similar in each case."

Farraday carefully cut a piece of the chicken in its dark sauce. "The gentleman in question," he continued, "was known to have arranged a rendezvous with an attractive woman who fled before the body was discovered. Similar incidents have occurred in several cities in South America and Mexico, and, most recently, in the U.S. Only two of the suspects were ever arrested. Both were in Los Angeles. One woman admitted to being a former prostitute, and both women, despite having been searched, managed to commit suicide with cyanide capsules before judicial proceedings could begin."

He paused and took a sip of the Chianti. "By the way, I love that shirt you're wearing. My mother used to have one like it." His gaze rested lightly on my face and upper body. "You look very beautiful. Your hair's longer. I like it. I hope you're enjoying this as much as I am. I've been looking forward to it . . . for a long time."

I felt a blush beginning in my face, which I hoped he would attribute to the wine. I was glad I'd chosen a simple black silk jacket and matching pants. I'd found my ivory lace shirt in a vintage clothing store in Seattle and never worn it before. "The coq au vin is excellent, Michael. And it's very nice to see you again." Slightly flustered at how much truth was contained in that sentence, I asked if either of the women arrested in L.A. had a panther tattoo.

"One had the panther on her right buttock, the other on the bottom of her right foot."

"Fortunately Andrea was not as secretive about the placement of her tattoo," I observed, "or I might never have put the pieces together."

Farraday watched thoughtfully as the waiter removed our plates, brushed a few nonexistent breadcrumbs from the tablecloth, and served raspberry trifle with coffee. "I hate to admit that I have not been able to find an answer your second question," he said slowly. "I checked with our man in Caracas to see if he could find any link between del Pino and the woman you know as Andrea de la Cruz. Officially, he knows nothing. Unofficially, his wife is a friend of a friend of del Pino's ex-wife, who divorced him five years ago, right after he was ambushed one night on his way home from the petroleum plant. He was shot in the shoulder." He shrugged. "It was no secret that del Pino and a number of his associates hated the administration. Perhaps somebody close to the president hired your pantera to eliminate del Pino, she tried and failed, he captured her and tamed her. Who knows?"

It was as good a tale as any other. And with Andrea in jail and Roberto del Pino *muerto*, it was purely academic. I considered the case closed. The person I did want to know more about was Michael Farraday, and what it was he wanted my "help" with. Again I studied him from beneath my lashes as he poured cream into his coffee, added one spoonful of sugar, and stirred slowly. In the three encounters I'd had with him during the sweetheart-swindler affair, I'd never seen him display anger or resort to intimidation. Even when he wasn't getting what he wanted. But there was a coiled energy about him—from the broad, muscled shoulders beneath the maroon silk shirt and well-tailored navy blazer to the equally well-muscled legs I'd observed the first time he visited my office. The fact that we'd ended up working together had been partly coincidental and partly because we shared a dogged determination to track down the wily MI6 agent who'd gone AWOL and left a trail of dead wives around the world.

"And now you want to know what I need your help with, don't you?" Farraday said.

I smiled. "I admit I'm intrigued."

"I had two motives in inviting you to meet me and both were selfish. The first was that I purely wanted to see you again and spend time with you. I won't ask you why you've been eluding me for a year and are now available. It's none of my business. However, I do have a project, we might call it, that I need your help with."

He glanced at my empty cup, refilled it from the well-polished silver pot without asking, and slid the cream pitcher toward me. "My brother, Donald, has had a more, shall we say, financially rewarding life than I. He's accumulated a number of toys around the world. In addition to his London house, he's just a bought a seaside villa in Majorca." He pulled two photographs from his left inside breast pocket. "This is Porto Sollér. Donald's house is the one farthest to the left." I examined the aerial shot of a cluster of whitewashed, red-tiled houses sprinkled over a hilltop surrounded on three sides by an azure sea. The second photo was of a sailboat in a brisk wind. "That's *Aphrodite*," he said. "Another of Donald's toys. A Swan 42."

Nautor Swan is the crème de la crème of sailing yachts. I'd probably sell a portion of my soul to sail on one. "She's beautiful."

He nodded. "Unfortunately, *Aphrodite* is in Lisbon, where Donald and his wife just sold a villa." I listened with rapt attention, afraid to speculate on where Farraday was going.

"Donald wants to get *Aphrodite* to Majorca as soon as possible, so he can entertain some of his Scottish golfing buddies there by the end of next month. He's adamant that he doesn't want to turn her over to a boat-delivery person. My sister-in-law is not keen on sailing, so I offered to help him sail her over. Incidentally," he said, "I've been sailing since I was a small tyke and I was commissioned in the Royal Navy."

"So you and Donald are taking *Aphrodite* to Majorca?" I tried to keep the envy out of my voice. "Sounds wonderful."

He shook his head. "That was the plan. Now it seems that Donald has a ferociously demanding schedule for the next fortnight." He paused, emptied his coffee cup, pushed the cup and saucer away, and looked at me with a quizzical grin. "So, Scotia MacKinnon, would you like to help me sail *Aphrodite* from Lisbon to Majorca? It's about a two-week trip and we can have the use of the house in Porto Sollér for a week after we arrive. If that's something that appeals to you. Oh, one more thing. Donald's in Seattle just now and has his company's Learjet at his disposal. We would need to leave tomorrow."

We took off from the Victoria airport with perhaps half an hour of daylight left. A full moon was rising in the east. Over Haro Straight, Farraday banked the little Cessna into a long arc to the northeast, over Roche Harbor and Spieden Island and then in a wide circle over Santa Maria. "I thought I'd like to get a look at the island that caused you so much grief. That all right?"

I nodded, frantically assembling a to-do list in my mind for the following morning, wondering what feats of magic I would have to perform to be ready to fly away to Seattle and on to Madrid. He banked the plane sharply and I gazed down at the cliff where Zoe's life had ended so precipitously. At Gus's little stable in the valley where three lives had almost been lost. At the rolling green meadow where the azure butterflies had hovered. Daylight was fading. I could just make out the golden stone facade of the Hotel Dei Fiori on the hillside above the small harbor. As Farraday completed the turn and headed for San Juan Channel and the lights of Friday Harbor, I thought I glimpsed a shadowy figure in the old courtyard. And in the meadow below the vineyard, a strange circle of white. What was that all about?

EPILOGUE

The new moon rose slowly above the tall Douglas firs that blackened in the fading light. Lazy dark clouds drifted over the forested hillside. The moon eluded the clouds and continued its ascent. On the western hillside across the valley, below the vineyard, the door of what had been the old convent opened. The tall figure of a man emerged. He crossed the courtyard, arranged two large cushions on the old stone banquette near the fountain where the sisters had always gathered after vespers, and opened a long, leather case.

The moon climbed higher and illuminated the courtyard in silvery light. The man lifted a bamboo flute to his lips and began to blow an old Japanese melody. The throaty tones floated in the evening air, drifted phantomlike across the valley. From somewhere in the shadows, a large cat leaped to the stone bench and sat on its haunches between the two cushions.

Below the courtyard, in a flat, grassy clearing that

was filling with a fine mist, a white antelope lifted
its head from the meadow grass where it had been
grazing in the twilight. Its ears lifted and it stared
in the direction of the music. As the notes of the
flute continued to drift across the darkening valley,
the white antelope was silently joined by another
of its kind. And then another.

In the courtyard above, a tall woman in a long
dress joined the flute player and the large cat on
the banquette. The first song of the flute ended. The
courtyard grew brighter with moonlight and the man
began another melody. An hour passed. The man put
down the flute, glanced down into the moonlit
meadow, rubbed his eyes. He touched the woman
softly on her shoulder and together they absorbed the
scene below where the circle of white antelope had
gathered, motionless, all staring uphill at the courtyard. Evening silence reclaimed the meadow. The
first antelope slowly turned and trotted gracefully
away into the darkness, followed one by one, in
single file, by the rest of the white herd.

A cool breeze rippled through the upper branches
of the fir trees. The scudding clouds overtook the
moon and a misty darkness cloaked the valley and
the hillside.

ACKNOWLEDGMENTS

The author wishes to thank the following individuals for their input to *The Lavender Butterfly Murders:* Dick Britten, Martin Garren, Jr., Island County Sheriff Michael Hawley, Michelle Kirsch, Mona Meeker, Dr. Richard Miller, Lainey Volk, Larry and Lyle Willson, and San Juan County Undersheriff Jon Zerby.

With special thanks to my editor, Ellen Edwards, for her suggestions on structure and content.

And with all due respect to the Sheriff's Departments of San Juan and Island Counties, the author begs forgiveness for taking outrageous liberties with local law enforcement procedures and personalities.